AMMUNITION UP
THE COMPLETE ADVENTURES OF CORDIE,
SOLDIER OF FORTUNE, VOLUME 5

AMMUNITION UP
THE COMPLETE ADVENTURES OF CORDIE, SOLDIER OF FORTUNE, VOLUME 5

W. WIRT

ILLUSTRATED BY
SAMUEL CAHAN

COVER BY
PAUL STAHR

POPULAR PUBLICATIONS · 2022

TABLE OF CONTENTS

AMMUNITION UP!

*When it came to fighting Japanese invaders,
even the famous Manchu Big Swords had a
lot to learn from Jimmie Cordie and his men*

1

ANAMESE SPY

THE JAPANESE HAD come south of the Great Wall, occupying among other cities, Nienyeun, on the Gulf of Fuchan. A good deal of foreign shipping was in port, but the Japanese had not bothered any of it. Japan was not at war with China—at least not officially—and any ship flying the flag of another nation had a perfect right to be there.

Many Chinese had left the city as the Japanese closed in, but there were still thousands who had stayed on. These had no reason to fear the Japanese occupancy, once the firing was over.

Like all Chinese cities, Nienyeun, below the surface of the ground, was a labyrinth of tunnels and rooms. Some of them below others, even to a third and fourth level. The Japanese intelligence and military police knew of this fact, in a general way, but paid no attention. They held the top of the ground and the harbor; and if the Chinese wanted to burrow like moles, they could help themselves, as far as the Japanese military was concerned.

Through one of these narrow, wet, evil-smelling tunnels on the second level there crawled a man. Literally crawled, his body dragging along the uneven dirt and rock floor. He had the use of his two hands and his right leg. The left leg seemed to be lifeless. His head and face were bloody where not caked with the slime of the passageway.

As he crawled, he whispered to himself, over and over: "Get to Jimmie—get—to—Jimmie. No—mustn't stop. Carry—on, carry on. You've got to make it, Carewe. You've got to—make it!"

At times the man fell forward on his chest and face and lay still for a moment. But as often as he did so, after a time he would go on.

John Cecil Carewe, ex-flight commander of a British air squadron and now an officer of the Big Swords, English gentleman and soldier of fortune, was wounded almost to death. In a tunnel under the Chinese city of Nienyeun, nevertheless, he carried on—as the Carewes have carried on for a thousand years, in England's battles and their own, on land and sea.

"Just a little further!" he coaxed himself, as one coaxes a tired child. "Just—a little—further. Must tell Jimmie that—that—"

He came to a turn, made it, lifted himself half way up, and fell against what looked like a wooden bulkhead. It

Jimmie Cordie drew his Colt in sudden alarm.

gave, and he fell with it into a room at least thirty feet square. As the crash came, a slim, wiry, black-eyed man, who was dressed as a Uryankhes Tartar, started. Jumping to his feet he voiced an oath. He stood beside a grim-faced Chinese. His swift drawing of a .45 Colt was fast, but it was equaled by the swiftness of the Chinese, as he drew a sword. A line of Chinese, reaching from a hole in the right wall of the room to another hole in the left wall, put down the cases which they were carrying. They also drew swords.

"Hold 'er, Jimmie!" Carewe said, a smile on his bloody lips. "I—I—"

Jimmie Cordie was an ex-sergeant of the Foreign Legion and captain of machine gun company, A.E.F., now the right-hand man of the Manchu noble, Chang-Lung Liang, who commanded the Big Swords. Jimmie reached Carewe before Carewe's head began to sink forward. He cradled Carewe's broken body in his arms.

"Steady, Jonathan! I've got you. You made it.—No, don't

"Hold it, Jimmie!" gasped Carewe through bloody lips.

go to sleep yet. Stay with it, old-timer. Carewe—tell me. It's Jimmie. You came to tell me something Tell me—Carewe."

Carewe opened his eyes, looked up at Jimmie, then smiled again. "Right, old dear. I—made it in spite of the giddy old— Look out for Wang Lu He is—he has told the—"

"Don't go yet, Carewe. Hang to it. Where is Wang Lu?"

"I say—can't hold on much longer, you know. He is—is in Hsai T'ang's place with an Anamese girl who is a Ja—a Japan— Carry on, Jimmie! I've—been proud to have—to have—"

His head fell back in the crook of Jimmie Cordie's arm.

Jimmie Cordie lowered Carewe gently to the ground and then stood up. In the Orient, Jimmie Cordie was generally referred to by the Chinese as "the black-eyed, always smiling one." But now there was no smile in his eyes, or on his lips, either.

"Go and get Wang Lu, little brother," he ordered the grim-faced Chinese. "I await him here. Send a messenger to the ship and to the junks to discontinue the loading until further orders. Concentrate the swords of the T'aip'ing in the places we planned."

Shih-kai, the war captain of the powerful T'aip'ing Society, saluted with his sword before he sheathed it. "As you order, honorable elder brother.—Come with me, Yzu. You also, Lao. And you—"

HALF AN HOUR later, a Chinese youth of about sixteen was pushed roughly to his knees, in front of Jimmie Cordie. He was an intelligent looking boy, dressed in the robes and cap of a student. On his face there was an expression which was partly fear and partly a determination to brazen things out.

Jimmie Cordie looked down at him. "What did you tell the Japanese spy, Wang Lu?"

"I—I do not know any spy of Nippon, honorable captain," answered Wang Lu, promptly. "I have talked to no one since we arrived."

Jimmie had spoken in Pushtu, the universal language of the border, and Wang Lu answered in the same.

"Except the Anamese girl. Who is she?"

"I do not know her very well. I met her at—"

"No, Wang Lu. Do not attempt to lie—with Captain Carewe there on the ground. I found you a year ago, in a deserted village far to the north. You were hungry and very cold. Do you remember, Wang Lu? I fed you and gave you warm clothes to wear, and made you my servant. Have you forgotten?—Now, once more, what did you tell the Japanese spy?"

"I have not forgotten anything. I—I told nothing to any Nippon spy. I was talking to the girl about—"

Jimmie Cordie held up his hand. "I haven't time to listen to lies, Wang Lu. Shih-kai, you will give this degraded one who bites at the hand who feeds him the death of the thousand cuts. Gag him so that his screams will not attract attention from beyond the passageways."

"No! No!—You dare not! The men of—I— Soon you will be—"

What Wang Lu was about to say was smothered by the sleeve of a robe being thrust into his mouth. Five second later, he was held with his back to the wall. T'aip'ing swordsmen held his arms and his legs in vise-like grips.

In front of him stood Shih-kai, his razor-sharp sword held seemingly loose. The death of a thousand cuts means that little by little a man's body is cut away. Few men have endured it without becoming, long before the count has reached twenty, cringing, begging things who will do anything to have the torture stop.

"You can move your head," Jimmie Cordie said, coldly. "When you are ready to tell me the truth, move it up and down once. Start, Shih-kai. I will count.—One—"

The razor-sharp sword darted up, and as it passed the Chinese boy's face, a small piece of an upper lip fell to the ground. A piece no bigger than the head of a shingle nail. **THAT WAS ALL** that was necessary. Wang Lu had thought that he was brave and could endure all things, that he was like a hero of old and could die like one if called upon to do it. But now, as he felt the sting of the cut, he realized all of a sudden that he was not a hero, and that he was not brave. He was only a Chinese boy in the hands of the dreaded T'aip'ing, who were about to torture him to death, unless....

Wang Lu nodded his head up and down; not once, but three or four times. As the gag was removed from his mouth and the holds on his arms and ankles released, he sank to his knees.

"*Aie! Aie!*" he wailed in Chinese. "Do not! Do not, mighty ones! I will tell! I will tell all!"

Shih-kai translated, for Jimmie Cordie did not understand much Chinese, hardly enough to give his few military commands. And when Jimmie spoke again, in English, Shih-kai put it in Chinese for the boy.

"Tell the truth," Jimmie commanded, "and do not seek

to evade or to lie. After that, it may be that I can stop the flow of blood so that you will not bleed to death. Now— what did you tell the Japanese spy?"

"I told her of the ship which is here, with ammunition for the Big Swords. And of your plan to cut a hole in the ship below the level of the wharf and so remove the ammunition at night, passing it along under the wharf. I told of the junks at the other wharf, waiting to receive it. I—mercy, resplendent one who rules the world! Do not look at me that way."

"WHAT ELSE DID you tell the Japanese spy?"

"I—I told of you and of Captain Carewe being here."

"You told of this room, and of the way to the junks?"

"Yes, mighty one."

"Did you tell the Japanese spy anything else?"

"No, nothing else."

"How long ago did you tell all this to the Japanese spy?"

"Two hours."

"Have you told any other Japanese spy anything?"

"No, I only met and told the Anamese girl and—"

"What happened to Captain Carewe?"

"I do not know, magnificent one."

"You told all this to the Japanese spy. Then what happened?"

"She left me, and I sat for some minutes, drinking wine. Then one came up to me and said that a man I knew wanted to see me in one of the back rooms. I went back, and—the T'aip'ing got me."

"I see. Well, because you have told the truth I will spare you the death of the thousand cuts. Shih-kai, take this degraded person to the junks and—"

Wang Lu had observed that a passageway was within five feet of him, to his left. As Shih-kai stepped forward, Jimmie Cordie stepped back, so clearing Wang Lu's way to the hole, if he threw himself at it. The roof of the hole was about four feet from the ground. He was fast, this Chinese boy; and now that his first scare was dying out, he tried for the hole. It was a foolish try, and one that few men would have attempted. But he was young, quick as a flash, and not given to thinking of the consequences of his acts.

But even as he made for the hole, a T'aip'ing swordsman leaned forward. A sword licked out like the tongue of a snake, and Wang Lu's body fell to the ground, literally cut in two pieces.

"Thank you, little brother," Jimmie Cordie said. "He made a good try—and lost. Shih-kai, order that the loading be stopped for— No, let it go on, but slowly. What I can't dope out, though, is why the Japs haven't struck, if they knew all this two hours ago—I just saw Carewe move! And I thought he had gone on High!"

Jimmie Cordie took up in his arms the slim body of the game English flyer. "Never mind about the little men of Nippon, war brother. Send the good swords of the T'aip'ing through all passageways up to the first level, and on both sides. Slay all who may be watching. I want a clear, unwatched path to the right."

2

LAUGHING-STOCK OF NIPPON

"**LET THE MONGRELS** who flouted us load the junks and sail with them. One of our destroyers will follow and sink them all. If the Yankee and the Englishman are not killed in the sinking by our shell fire, they will be taken from the water, and after being questioned they will face a firing squad. That is all, gentlemen."

Two Japanese military intelligence officers and a military police officer saluted as Colonel Nagayo of the intelligence finished speaking. That was all they could do. Colonel Nagayo rated them, and was, as they knew, more than impatient of advice or suggestion. Privately, the three officers thought that the Big Sword officers and the T'aip'ing who were unloading the ammunition and the steamer and the junks should be taken at once, whenever and wherever found. But Colonel Nagayo was very close to Lieutenant General Yiabu of the High Command. So they saluted and marched out of headquarters.

Once on the street, the military police officer excused himself. Major Mito, of the intelligence, said: "I am going to a place where I hope to get further information, Captain Choshi. Do you wish to come with me, or do you prefer to familiarize yourself with Nienyeun and the water front?"

"I much prefer to stay with you, major, if you will permit me to. As you know, I have just arrived from Tokyo and all things here are new to me. Many things puzzle me."

"I will be glad to, Captain Choshi. What puzzles you most?"

"Two things, major. First, just who are the Big Swords? We heard much about them in Nippon, but it was all vague information."

"When our troops first occupied Manchuria—or I should say, Manchukuo—there were, in various parts of the territory to the northwest, bands of masterless men of all breeds. They were led by ex-Chinese war lords, so called. Ex-generals whose armies had been destroyed, they were; bandits and tribesmen. In short, a collection of mongrels. They had but few guns, and so they fought with the sword for a weapon. Hence the name, Big Swords. Is that plain to you, Captain Choshi?"

"Yes, major. It is very plain."

"Very well. That was the situation when our Eighth Division took Lueh, in the Nonni River area. There the family of a Manchu noble named Chang-Lung Liang, Head of the House of Chi, was slain. This proud noble, who thinks that all races are far beneath the Manchu, was in the south when it happened. He came to the north and swore on the golden scroll of the House of Chi that he and all men of the House of Chi would devote the rest of their lives to the slaying of, as he called us, 'the little men of Nippon.' It is too long a story to tell at the moment, Captain Choshi. Suffice it to say that he organized the Big Swords into a compact body, putting many of the leaders to the sword in doing it.—Now the Big Swords are under an iron discipline, and they are armed with modern weapons."

"**HOW MANY OF** them are there, major?"

"Our reports state that at the moment there are some twenty-odd thousand, captain. By that I mean shock troops. There were a good many more, but"—the Japanese officer smiled coldly—"once in a while we trap and destroy detachments of them. Since the Manchu Chang-Lung Liang took them over, I will frankly admit, they have been as a thorn in our sides. If we send sufficient force to wipe them out, they retreat into the mountains and raise the Uryankhes and Altai Tartars against us. Once in the hills, of course, a few can hold off many, Captain Choshi. Does that explain the Big Swords to you?"

"Yes, very clearly. Thank you, major.—Now, if you will be so kind, what is it about the American and English soldiers of fortune who fight for the Big Swords? I mean, why is the intelligence and the military police so bitter against them?"

"Did you not hear in Tokyo what happened in Tsitihar? I mean to us of the intelligence and the military police?"

"Why, I heard a little, major. There was some talk about the Big Swords taking a prisoner away, and—I was very busy on other matters, so—"

"Well, this I will tell you, Captain Choshi. The Big Swords, led by the soldiers of fortune, came into Tsitihar during a blizzard; and by a trick, they took military police headquarters. Then they took the military prison where we had put a prisoner. After which they seized an armored train and fled to the north with it. Thus we became the laughing-stock of the army."

"Now I understand why Colonel Nagayo wished them

to think that they had succeeded in getting away with the ammunition."

"That is it, Captain Choshi. We hold them in the hollow of our hands.—And this I also know; our seventh division—all of it—is moving to the northwest, with orders to clear of the Big Swords all territory up to and including the Thian Shan range."

"But why have they suddenly become of so much importance that an entire division must be sent against them?"

Major Mito laughed. "The Big Swords themselves do not rate a division, captain. But—the Red Dogs do. When the Reds start through the ranges, there must be no Big Swords or Uryankhes and Altai Tartars to assist them. They will find that Nippon guns command the passes."

"Thank you for telling me, Major Mito. Then the division goes up to—shall I say—sweep the territory of the Thian Shan, clean?"

"That is correct, captain. I go tonight to watch the loading of the junks. Do you wish to go with me?"

"I would like to very much. But how can you get close enough to watch? If you are taken, they will know that we are aware of their plans." Captain Choshi was plainly concerned over the risks his superior officer was planning to take.

"They think that the wharf, the shops and the houses near, and all the underground passages are guarded by T'aip'ing swords. It may be that they are, but I know a place from which we both can watch."

3

SOLDIERS OF FORTUNE

THE CHINESE VILLAGE of Chautin was on the right bank of the River Fengning, which rises in the Ulenna Range and empties into the Gulf of Fuchan. At Chautin, the river is about a mile wide, and the current is swift.

The village had been an unloading place for stuff going to the north and west. After the Japs arrived in Manchukuo, there had been very little unloading, and most of the villagers had fled. It had been built on flat ground, exposed to attack on three sides; on all four if the attackers used the river. In the old days, of course, the swordsmen of the war lord in whose territory the village was were able to stop with his swordsmen any enemy at the boundary lines.

When a Big Swords unit of about two thousand men arrived at Chautin, the American soldiers of fortune who commanded with the Manchu nobles of the House of Chi took one look at the terrain and shook their heads. As far as they knew, there were no Japanese troops of any force within fifty or sixty miles, and those near were defending strategic points. But that did not mean that the Big Swords were safe from attack, once it became known that a large force of them had camped at Chautin.

About a mile below the village there was a rough and

rocky island in the middle of the river. The river forked, ran alongside, then closed again at the south end of the island. On either side of the island there was, roughly, three-eighths of a mile of water. At one time—it might have been a thousand years ago—the island had been used as a place of worship, or as a training ground for priests or warriors.

Once upon this island, defense was easy. Even from air attack there was plenty of cover made by rocks falling on top or across each other, so forming great chambers. All the bombs the Japs had in Manchukuo could not reach through a hundred feet of solid rock. Moreover, long ago a massive stone pier had been run out into the river from the island, on the side that faced the mainland where the village of Chautin was located. This pier was still in good condition, and was about two hundred feet long. Old as it was, the swift current of the river, pushing against the pier, had worn away hardly a foot of it.

In places where the rocks gave clearance, there were a few stone houses; and on top of one of the rocks, in a place where the river could be seen on both sides, was a massive, squat building, with ornately carved sides. This structure had been a temple or council house. The only way to get up to it was by a path hewn out of the rock on the side looking down the river.

ONE OF THE soldiers of fortune, standing with two Manchu officers, looked at Chautin and said:

"We can't stay here. Captain Cordie told me of an island a mile below Chautin, a place that would be an easy place to hold indefinitely. We'll go down and look it over."

The speaker was George Grigsby, born in the Kentucky

hills, ex-Legionnaire, and major of infantry, A.E.F. A big, lean-flanked, broad-shouldered man with a clean-cut, Anglo-Saxon face, and one of the most famous soldiers of fortune in the East.

"What you say is true, elder brother," one of the Manchus answered. "We cannot stay here. It may be that Captain Cordie will be delayed in bringing up the ammunition. We will go and look at the island, as you say." He spoke in Pushtu, of course, which is the language of the border.

"We may as well move the detachment down," Grigsby said. "Get going, Yang Chu."

Orders were shouted. A red-headed man, fully as tall as Grigsby, and much more burly, was sitting near a machine gun company. He said to a short, very broad-shouldered man whose face was distinctly Semitic: "What the hell, now? This is Chautin, ain't it, ye Yid monkey-faced duck? Are we to go walkin' after comin' five hundred miles on the feet ave us?"

The man who spoke was Red Dolan, known wherever adventurers gather as "that red-headed wild man from Cork." Ex-Foreign Legion, and lieutenant of military police in France; two hundred and thirty pounds of fighting Irish. Since the day when he had met Jimmie Cordie in the Legion, life had become simplified for Red.

The Fighting Yid stretched as he rose, and grinned. "All de Dolans have got it veak feet—und veak heads also. Vant poppa to carry you, little von? Sure, dis is Chautin! but it don't look good to George.—Ve go hunt us some place else to rest de veary bones! Up and at 'em, Irish bum!"

The Yid, born on Hester Street, New York City, and named Abraham Cohen, was just about as broad as he was long, and looked as if he were fat. Yet the Yid was all bone and muscle. The surprised look which was perpetually on his face was more than misleading, for the Yid was never surprised at anything. As first sergeant of Jimmie Cordie's machine gun company in France, he received the name of Fighting Yid.

"SEE THAT!" RED demanded, mournfully. "See that, Codfish! Here I was, talkin' to this Yid beneath notice, all nice and friendly; and what does the benighted scut ave the world do? He makes a di-ert-ty crack about the Dolans.— Listen to me, ye potbellied gibbon! Wan Dolan, if he had weak feet on him—which no Dolan ever had—could chase all the Yids from hell to breakfast, and so far that—"

A tall, lanky man who had been sitting on an ammunition case, interrupted. "Just who was this one Dolan you are always talking about, Terrence Aloysius, me good man? All the Dolans I ever saw couldn't do much more than push a paper doll over."

This was the Boston Bean, born in Boston, Massachusetts, and listed in the Social Register as John Cabot Winthrop. Ex-Foreign Legion and captain of artillery, A.E.F. His face was always mournful and grave looking, but that mournful, grave look was as misleading as the Yid's look of surprise. The Bean was reckless and happy-go-lucky to the nth degree.

If one asked, in China, "Do you know where John Cabot Winthrop is?" the answer, nine times out of ten, would be a curt, "Don't know him." But if the question were worded, "Where is the Boston Bean?" or "Where is the Codfish?" the answer would be, "He's up in the north with Jimmie Cordie," or "He and the Yid are down in Tonkin."

"Wan Dolan," Red repeated firmly, "can lick all the Yids and all the long-legged cranes from Bosting put together! I'll show ye, ye half baked—"

"Put it off for a little while," the Bean interrupted. "I better get to the battery. We're next."

Grigsby, Red, the Yid and the Bean stood on the bank of the river and looked across at the island.

"Well," the Bean said, "if we can find an open place over there large enough to sit down on we can certainly make it darned unpleasant for any unwelcome callers."

"Dot's easy!" the Yid answered. "Make it rafts, und start dem off from de shore about half a mile up. Den let de current—"

"Who the hell ever slapped ye in the kisser wid a transit and told ye that ye was an engineer, ye pink-tailed monkey?" demanded Red scornfully. "Wid George and the Codfish Duke here, are ye to be listened to? Ye are not!—Back away and let good men get at it."

"You being von of dem, I suppose? Vot de—"

"Both of you put a jaw tackle on," Grigsby interrupted. "The Yid was offering help, Red. Let's figure this thing out without a lot of wah-wah from you two. Save it until after we get over there."

4

BOMBED

THE BIG SWORDS did what the Yid suggested, and reached the island safely, horses, guns, ammunition, quartermaster stores and all, without the loss of a man or a piece of equipment. It was a long job, and at times a hard one; but the Big Swords had crossed rapidly flowing rivers before. The soldiers of fortune, whom the Big Sword rank and file held to be "honorable elder brothers," made the crossing a game.

Once over, places were found that could not be seen from the river bank, and in an hour the Big Swords were ready to "Resist it boarders, ain't it?" as the Yid put it.

Grigsby, the Bean, the Yid and Red moved into the old stone temple, or what-not, up on top of the great rock. It contained a single, large room, and a little better than half way up, a gallery that ran around all sides. Smaller rooms opened off the gallery on either side. At the front and rear, instead of these smaller rooms, there were two larger ones, which ran across the width of the entire temple.

There was no furniture or anything else in any of the rooms, and the windows consisted of narrow slits cut through the stone wall, one for each small room, and four in each of the big rooms.

Red had been looking out of one of the slits, when the sound of airplane motors was heard. They all ran out of the temple and looked up. Coming from the east were four planes.

"I think," the Boston Bean said gravely, "we have arrived home in the well-known nick of time. Those are—"

"Get your outfits under cover!" Grigsby ordered as he started down the rock. "They are Japanese bombers. Snap into it, you birds!"

"Birds is good," the Yid said, as he and the Bean ran. "De birds is up dare. Ve are de groundhogs dot dey—"

"The *what?* Do you class yourself as a hog, my distinguished friend from Hester Street? Double shame on you for ever thinking about— Here they come down. Let out another link of speed, Mr. Groundhog, or you'll be the one with wings."

The Japanese planes swooped down, flew close over the island, came back, scattered out a little. This time they cut loose the heavy T.N.T. bombs.

But the Big Swords were officered by men who took no chances that could be avoided. Every unit was placed so that in case of an air raid, they could get to cover within a few moments. The horses were already safely housed in stables ready made by mother nature. Stables that had roofs of fifty feet or more of solid rock. The machine guns and the one- and two-pound rapid fire, and the mountain battery, were all placed close to cover. The stores, too, had been put away under the thick stone roof. Before the Jap planes had passed over the island for the second time, there was nothing in the open, except those Big Swords who were close enough to dive into a funk hole when the bombing started.

THE YID AND the Bean, whose battery was next to the Yid's machine guns as the first bomb started down, holed together. Red had his private hole, on the other side of the machine guns, which he commanded with the Yid.

"My!" the Yid said, as the detonations came. "Lucky ve vasn't at Chautin, ain't it, Codfisher?"

"Darn right it is, Mr. Cohen! Move over a little. Your Colt is sticking in my— Hear that! Heavy artillery! I wonder what made us so popular all of a sudden. Generally, our boy friends have with them a few machine guns and what-not when they come calling on us!"

"Listen to dot!—My, such a vaste of powder. I speak to the Mick-a-doo de next time I get it to Tokyo."

"Yeah? Say, you're due for a trip to the hot place, first. I have a feeling that we are— It's stopped. Let's take a look-see."

When they got to a place where they could see both sides of the mainland, the Yid said, "Look, Beany! On both sides—they sent it a division to get us dis time."

The Yid exaggerated a little. There was not a division in sight, though there were plenty of Japanese troops and artillery. The Seventh Division, on its way to the Thian Shan, had received word from its spies that there was a large body of Big Swords near Chautin. The commander had detached a part of the division to go over and destroy the Big Swords. And the planes had spotted the Big Swords on the island.

"They stand there looking us over," the Bean drawled, "as if we were a—"

A Big Sword bugle blew the order to "Commence firing! Commence firing!"

"Dot's de boy, George!" the Yid shouted, as his machine gunners began popping up out of holes with their beloved guns. The Bean ran for his battery.

From the right and left shores of the island, a sleet of steel-jacketed bullets, and several one- and two-pound high explosive shells as well as shells from the mountain battery, came on the Japanese troops. It was accurate, deadly fire. Jimmie Cordie and the others had spent much time, and even more ammunition, teaching the young Manchu nobles of the House of Chi how to operate machine and rapid fire guns. The mountain battery had been—and still was—the Boston Bean's pet.

THE JAPANESE STOOD it for a moment or so, and then their bugles began to blow. The Japanese did not retreat, but they executed one of their famous "rearward movements," and it was executed with all promptness. The banks cleared as if by magic, and immediately afterward the Japanese guns opened up. But they were back some distance from the point where the "rearward movement" had started.

The Big Sword bugle blew "Cease firing—cease firing," and a moment later, "Officers front and center."

"Vare de hell is it, front und center?" the Yid asked.

Red answered, "Wherever George is, ye hook-nosed rookie! Ye don't know nawthin', do ye?"

"I know it dot I kick it de slate loose from a Irish *gonif*, ven I get it a minute's time."

"Come on," called the Bean, as he passed. "What do you think this is, an old ladies' home? Bring your tatting with you!"

"My!" the Yid said. "It is gettin' so dot two friends can't even say it von word mit unless—"

The bugle blew again, and this time it sounded impatient. "Officers front and center! Officers front and center!"

The Yid laughed. "Come on, ye red-headed bummer. Ve vill be late for de school."

Grigsby looked at the officers standing with him under a rock shelf; the young, alert, intelligent Manchus of the House of Chi, the Chinese who had been in command of the independent bands that had joined the Big Swords, and who had fought their way up to the command of regiments; the several Cossacks and Tartars; at the Yid, the Bean and Red Dolan.

"The only way they can get over here is to come down on rafts, the way we did," Grigsby said. "Place your guns so they command the river from the north end of the island. Keep your infantry under cover until the time comes to use it. No needless exposure. The guns can keep them off until the ammunition is exhausted. After that, your swords can take the matter up where the guns leave off, Yang Chu. That's all. Move out, gentlemen."

"Ve got to do more dan stand it off de Japs," the Yid said, as he and Red went back to the machine guns. "Ve got to chase it dem back into de tall uncut. Oddervise, ven Jimmie comes mit de ammunition, dey gather him in."

"Holy Saint Peter!" Red shouted, " 'Tis so, Abie, darlin'! Go on to the guns. I'll go back and ask George about it."

5

HONORABLE ELDER BROTHER

JIMMIE CORDIE AND Shih-kai sat in a room in the house of Hokian, a Chinese merchant of Nienyeun. They had gained entrance to the room through an underground passageway. Carewe was now in bed, a Chinese doctor attending him.

"My honorable elder brother, the healer tells me that your war brother has a chance to live—but a very slim one, Captain Cordie," Hokian said. "How did it happen that he has become like a broken twig?"

"I don't know, Hokian. I wish I did. All I know is this…."

Hokian listened, his fat old face impassive. He was one of the richest merchants in northern China. As he listened, he must have known that if his connection with the Big Swords became known to the Japanese, he would face a firing squad, but there was nothing in his eyes or on his face to show that he knew it, or cared.

After Jimmie had finished telling what had happened, he went on. "I knew of no other place to bring Captain Carewe but here, elder brother. The Lord Chang-Lung Liang ordered me to contact you on arrival at Nienyeun, stating that if help were needed, you would furnish it. I contacted you as ordered, and you showed me the way into your house from the ground. Now I have used it in a way that I did not think I would ever have to. In so doing, I have endangered you, if the presence of Captain Carewe becomes known. I do not know how far you can or will go for the Lord—"

Hokian interrupted, something the Chinese seldom do. "Know this, Captain Cordie. All I have, my life included, belongs to the Manchu Lord, Chang-Lung Liang. Why, in no way concerns the matter in hand. I ask that you take it for granted. You have a plan?"

"I have a more or less half-baked one that depends on quite a few 'ifs,' Hokian. I am going on the assumption that the Japanese do not know that Captain Carewe has warned me. Had he been in their hands it is hardly possible that he could have escaped without help. And there are none here to help him but the T'aip'ing and me. I think that on the way to me he must have run into trouble of some kind and fought his way through. What makes me believe it more strongly is the fact that the Japanese had some two hours to close in before the warning reached me."

"Your reasoning, Captain Cordie, is the reasoning of a clever, alert brain. Given that what you think is so, what then?"

Hokian was speaking Chinese, and Jimmie Cordie English, Shih-kai translating.

"WELL, HOW DO you stand with the Japanese?"

"I have traded with the men of Nippon for a good many years, and am well known to them. I did not leave the city before they arrived, and since then I have furnished supplies when called upon to do so. I am—shall I say—classed as a friend of Nippon. Many of the higher Japanese officers here are of families who are in my debt—my trade debt—and I have never forced payment."

"Then any request of yours would stand a good chance of being granted?"

"If the request is a proper one to make, under the circumstances, and if I can show a reason or reasons for asking it, yes."

"That's one of the 'ifs'—I will tell you what is forming in my mind.—It may be that you and Shih-kai can help mature it. I now speak my thoughts as they come to me."

"May I ask you a question before you begin to speak your thoughts, Captain Cordie? I know that the honorable Shih-kai is a war captain of the mighty, all-powerful T'aip'ing. And yet, he obeys you, an American soldier of fortune, and he calls you 'honorable elder brother.' Will you explain why, Captain Cordie?"

"I will," answered Jimmie, with a grin. "The only son of Yen Yuan, Head of the T'aip'ing, was, quite a few years ago, a student in America. I also was a student at the same school. I knew him only as a clever, likable Chinese youth named Singan. One day I learned that he had contracted a virulent, contagious fever and had been taken to a hospital. He was a stranger in a strange land and I knew how he must feel.

"So I went to the hospital and succeeded in getting in to him, staying beside him until he was once more well and strong. Years afterward I met Singan by chance in Hong Kong. He took me to his father, Yen Yuan, and I was introduced as the one who had saved Singan's life. Which was not strictly true, of course, but I could not make either Yen Yuan or Singan believe it. Yen Yuan announced that I was his honorable elder brother, and word went through the T'aip'ing to that effect. Ever since I have been honored and obeyed, although I am not a member of the society, Hokian."

"I thank you for the explanation, Captain Cordie. And now—for the plan."

6

JAPANESE INTELLIGENCE

"**THE LAST OF** the ammunition, and several cases that must have held machine and rapid fire guns, was loaded on the T'aip'ing junks last night," Major Mito reported to Colonel Nagayo, early one morning. "As we left our observation post, they were getting ready to sail. Truly, they were careless about the loading. At first, the cases were carried on board under fishing nets and other gear, but toward the last they carried them up over the wharf quite openly."

"You are very foolish if you hold the T'aip'ing so lightly, Major Mito, that you believe them guilty of carelessness."

"I do not hold them lightly, Colonel Nagayo. I brought in a high-pooped junk to the next wharf, and through a hole I watched—"

"I do not care for the details, major.—So, the 'honorable elder brother' of the mighty Head," Colonel Nagayo said, sardonically, "now sails to his death. Also, the T'aip'ing will be taught that it is not wise to lift its head too far from the ground when it strikes at us. Soon we will be able to—"

An intelligence officer came in, with him an old Chinese woman. In his hand he carried a package wrapped in a cloth.

"What is the meaning of this intrusion, Lieutenant

Akita?—You dare to bring this hag into my presence unsummoned? Learn that such things are not done!"

"The urgency must by my excuse, colonel.—Look at this."

He unwrapped the package. In his hand was a machine gun belt, full of cartridges. He advanced to Colonel Nagayo's desk and put the belt on it.

Colonel Nagayo picked it up. "Browning ammunition!" he exclaimed. "Where was it found? What has this old woman to do with it?"

"She was seen coming from a certain place with it in her hands, and was halted by one of our men, who turned her over to the military police. I was there, and after hearing her story, I brought her to you." Then, in Chinese, he said to the old woman, "Tell the Ruler of the World who sits at the table all about it, old mother of many sons. Do not be afraid. He will not punish you if you tell the truth. Instead, you will be greatly enriched."

It was a long, rambling story which the old woman told in her shrill, quavering voice. All in all, it amounted to this: her daughter was a servant of Hokian, the merchant, and two nights ago she had suddenly been sent to Hokian's country place.

The old woman lived with her daughter, and last night her daughter's youngest child had cried a long time. She wanted her doll, the one her grandmother had made for her out of rags. The child's mother told the little girl that the doll must remain where it was until they returned to Nienyeun, but the child cried so hard.

So hard, in fact, that she, the old grandmother, had decided to slip into Nienyeun, go to Hokian's house under cover of the darkness, get the doll, and slip out. She knew that Hokian had given strict orders that none were to come back until he ordered them to, but—and so on.

The Japanese intelligence let her ramble along, not even asking questions. That could come later.

SHE HAD MADE it to the house, and to her great surprise, she found it vacant. No one there, and all the household goods removed. She found the doll on a pile of rubbish, and started back to tell the news to her daughter and all the other servants who had been sent to the country. Then she thought that she would go to the warehouse and see if she could find a piece of cloth or some other valuable thing that had been discarded.

She got into the warehouse through a hole in the wall, and looked around.

There were several piles of bags, besides great piles of beans, vegetables and seeds. And in pawing around, she had found the belt of little shining metal objects. She had taken the belt for one of her grandsons.

She had meant to do no wrong, and she hoped the resplendent Ruler of the World would pardon her.

"You did right bringing her here," Colonel Nagayo said. "Take her out, Lieutenant Akita, and see to it that she is paid fifty yen, on my order."

The young lieutenant's face fell. He had wanted to be in the know, but an order had been given, so he merely saluted, and led the old woman away.

Colonel Nagayo sat at his desk, his face grim. He stared at the belt of cartridges. Major Mito and Captain Choshi, who were also there, sat quite still, their eyes on the colonel.

Suddenly Nagayo laughed. "And I had just finished

saying that the 'honorable elder brother' of the mighty Head sails to his death. Instead, I go to the shrine of my ancestors, and there I commit hara-kiri."

"But—but why?—I do not understand what you mean, Colonel Nagayo."

"Do you not, major?—What is that?" He pointed to the belt.

"That is a belt of Browning machine gun ammunition, colonel."

"Correct. And who uses Brownings in Manchukuo?— No wonder you are still only a major."

Major Mito sprang to his feet. "The Big Swords!"

"Again you are correct. Yesterday, the Chinese merchant Hokian asked Lieutenant General Yiabu for permission to go to the north, with his household goods and all else that he had here in Nienyeun. He stated that he had called one of his ships up from the south to transport him. Permission was readily granted, after I had been asked if the intelligence knew of any reason why the move should be prevented. I had reported that the intelligence knew of no reason why the Chinese merchant Hokian should not be allowed to go to the north if he so desired. And now—and now—"

"But we *saw* the ammunition being loaded on the junks!"

"Did you?—Or did you see merely the ammunition cases, probably filled with dirt? Here is what has happened, Major Mito. Somewhere between the ships and the junks, the ammunition was taken from the cases and dirt or rocks put in. Then the ammunition was taken to Hokian's house, and there put in sacks—the sacks that held the beans and seeds. Some careless worker dropped an ammunition belt,

and before it was seen and picked up, a sack was acciden-
tally kicked or dropped over it."

"But—it may be that the belt got to Hokian's house in
some other way. One of the bearers may have stolen it, or—
There are many ways in which it could have reached there."

Colonel Nagayo had risen to his present rank by his
cleverness, and not by pull. He smiled wearily.

"You think so? Go to the junks and search them. You will
find neither ammunition and the guns, nor the T'aip'ing.
The loading you witnessed last night was probably done by
local Chinese who by now have also disappeared."

He called a number on the phone, and after a moment
asked, "Has the Lao-Tzu, belonging to the merchant
Hokian, yet sailed?" Receiving an answer, he hung up.
"The Lao-Tzu sailed last night at eight o'clock, clearing
for Takushan."

"Then we can take her there! It will be the same as if we
took the junks," Captain Choshi said.

"She will not go there, captain. She will meet some other
ship and will transfer the ammunition or put in at some
unknown harbor where— Get to the junks, Major Mito. I
will order every plane and destroyer we have out to search
for the Lao-Tzu. It may be that we can find her before she
unloads. I will not think of hara-kiri yet."

Inside of an hour Major Mito reported back that the
cases were filled with dirt, all save a hundred and twenty,
which were on the bottom layer, in one of the junks. Also
that the junks were deserted.

7

FOX HUNT

CAREWE, WHO WAS sitting propped up in bed in the captain's cabin of the Lao-Tzu, smiled as Jimmie Cordie came in. The Lao-Tzu, under forced draft, was just entering the mouth of the Fengning River.

"How are you feeling now, Jonathan?" Jimmie asked, as he sat down.

"Quite all right, old dear. That giddy Chinese doctor must be a wizard—what, what, what!"

"I guess he learned most of his wizardry at the London City Hospital, old kid. At least he graduated from there."

"I say, Jimmie, tell me what happened. The last thing I remember before wakin' up on this jolly old hooker was seein' you draw down in the rat hole."

"Well, the doctor said we could talk for five minutes.— First, what happened to you?"

"I was comin' out of a place where I'd been lappin' up a couple of drinks with a ship captain I knew, and as I walked along a hall I glanced into one of the little drinkin' rooms."

"Wasn't the door shut?"

"How could I see in it if it were, old thing?—As I passed, a waiter came out with a tray. He did not close the door after him, and I glanced in, not thinkin' of anything special.

There was Wang Lu, talkin' to a girl. I knew her, Jimmie.
That is, I knew who she was. Down in Tonkin, they exposed
her as a Japanese spy, and she barely got away with her life.
I went to the end of the hall, then turned and came back.
When I got as far as the room, the door had been closed."

"What did you go to the end of the hall for?"

"The waiter was on my flamin' heels. I went so as to
shake him off before goin' back.—I say, if you ask all these
questions, old dear, our five minutes will be up before—"

"I beg your pardon," Jimmie answered, with a grin. "I am
naturally of an inquisitive mind. Proceed."

"Well, I went back; and by luck, the next room was
empty. So I nipped into it and closed and locked the door.
You know how thin the partition is between those rooms
in a drinkin' place. I put the old ear to the partition, but
I couldn't hear very much. Then I heard, 'Big Swords'
and 'Captain Cordie' and 'ammunition' and 'T'aip'ing'
and what-not.—Enough to tell me that Wang Lu was
unbeltin'."

"Darned lucky for us that your classic mug isn't known
to the Japs, and that you could wander around on top of
the ground as an English newspaper correspondent.—So
then what?"

"Why—I started for you, of course. I got lost underground, after I went through the passage from Ning's shop;
and all of a sudden I came into a room where there were
five or six Chinese holdin' some kind of a giddy meetin'.
I started to back out, but they didn't seem to want me to
leave them so quickly. It was a regular fox hunt! Every once
in a while one of the blighters would catch me. I didn't
want to shoot, but after I'd got messed up a bit, I had to. I

was afraid the Japs might hear the shots and begin investigatin'."

"I see. And you took an awful beating, so as not to imperil us."

"I say, that's rot—what, what! I took it because I thought I could handle the muckers without—"

"Yeah, I know, Jonathan. So finally you mopped up on all the chasers, and found your way to me."

"That's quite right, old chap. I came to a place I knew, and from then on I was all right."

"I NOTICE YOU were 'all right' when you arrived!" Jimmie answered, with a grin. "A little dirty, but quite all right. Well, that's that!—Now, acting on your tip, we first got Wang Lu, made him confess, and to cut a long story short, switched the ammunition to Hokian's house. Hokian got permission to leave for the north, with all his outfit, on one of his steamers. The Japs had no suspicion of him in any way.

"We put dirt in the ammunition cases, and kept right on loading the junks.—I'll fill in the details for you later.—After the ammunition and guns were on board the Lao-Tzu, in bean sacks and what-not, and stuck in hollow places in the furniture, you were carried on board as one of Hokian's women who was sick. Shih-kai and I and the T'aip'ing swords went on board disguised as Hokian's servants.

"The Japs paid no attention to the loading at all. So—here you are, on board the Lao-Tzu. And the ammunition is also on board, and we are yorricks and away for the Big Swords who wait at Chautin.—Now go to sleep," he ordered.

"Wait a minute, Jimmie! Didn't the Japs search the passageways for you?"

"I don't know. Maybe they did and we were too deep underground for them. We didn't catch any of them on the level. We used a cut-out place about a hundred feet from the ship to do the switching. Up to that place, and from there to the junks, we saw no Japs, Mr. Carewe. Next time I see a Jap intelligence officer I'll ask him about it."

"If they find out about Hokian, they'll follow the Lao-Tzu and—"

"If they do—yes. I don't think they will. It's catching before hanging, young fellow. Get to sleep now."

8

LITTLE MEN OF NIPPON

GRIGSBY WAS TALKING to some of the Manchus when Red came up.

"George, what about Jimmie comin' wid the ammunition? We got to run the little banties away from here. If we stay here playin' wid 'em, Jimmie will come sailin' up wid de—"

Grigsby asked gravely, "Can you suggest any way that we can start running them back, Red?"

"What? What the hell do I care how we run them, the little pink-toed scuts! Figure some way out, George. If Jimmie was here, he'd think up—"

"But he isn't, Red. Don't kid yourself, old-timer. Even if we were on the mainland, we couldn't run them. There are too many of them. If we can keep them off the island, we'll—"

"And let Jimmie come up to a trap? Up the river he'll come, all happy and content, thinkin' he is goin' to meet us; and—"

"Turn off that damn keening," Grigsby interrupted, curtly. "He's nowhere near here yet. Jimmie can look out for himself—all the time. We've got all we can do to keep our own scalps where they ought to be. Get back to your guns, Red."

"Sorry the day, George Grigsby, that I hear ye say you do not give a damn about Jimmie Cordie, and thinkin' about saving the scalp ave ye! Jimmie is—"

"Listen, you big red-head. Before we can save his, we have to save our own, haven't we? He's miles away from here, and the Japs are within half a mile of us."

" 'Tis right ye are, George. I know that ye love—"

"I do. I double love him.—Yeah, I thought so.—Here they come. Get to your guns, Red."

The Japanese, like the Big Swords, had figured out that the best way to get to the island was by starting rafts from above. The rafts which the Big Swords had used had been pulled up on the rocky shore of the island, but it did not take the Japs long to duplicate them.

As they appeared, loaded with infantry carrying bayoneted rifles and machine guns, the Japanese big guns on either shore opened up on the island. The planes came over, too, dropping bombs. But as the rafts neared the island, the muzzles of machine and rapid fire guns appeared from among the rocks. The rafts were cleared of men in less than a minute, and the muzzles of the guns then disappeared.

The Japanese bombardment had lifted as the rafts got close to the island. Now, as the empty rafts floated down, it began again, this time with increased intensity.

"Sounds as if dey is good und mad at us!" the Yid said, cheerfully. He, with Red, had retired to their hole-up.

"What the hell do we care what the likes ave them are!" demanded Red, who was worried about Jimmie Cordie.

"All they are is a lot ave bambalam midgets. We oughta go over there and slap 'em to hell outa the way."

"Oi, such a business! Dey could do it to us vot ve just did to dem. Vy should ve did it, I esk you? Here dey got to come und get us, vich is—"

"How about Jimmie, ye cross between a—?"

THE BOSTON BEAN slid down into the hole with them. He had decided to go and see Red and the Yid, and a little thing like a rain of steel meant nothing in his life.

"Gimme room, according to my size and disposition," he ordered as he hit the ground.

"Give ye nawthin', ye Bosting brown-bread eater!" growled Red. "Why the hell don't ye stay wid yer own outfit?"

"Our little Terrence Aloysius appears to be peeved at something. What is it, Mr. Cohen?"

"De big Irish bum is worried about Jimmie—vich is vot I call zero in vorryink. All de time, he does nothing but moan 'How about Jimmie?—How about Jimmie?' like a sick pussy-cat. Maybe more like it a sick cow.—Dot's it, a sick cow!"

"Aw—go to hell, both ave ye! If it was wan ave ye dish-faced gibbons, small worryin' would I be doin'. I'd be hopin' to hell the little men got ye. Lay off me in me sorrow, or I'll—Get outta the way, Codfish!"

For the Japanese had sent more rafts down. There was some heavy timber just above Chautin. It lined the banks of the river, and this time the Japs had erected on the rafts heavy breastworks about five feet high, on the sides fronting the island. Over the breastworks could be seen the points of bayonets. The rafts, two or three times as many as in the first try, seemed to be tied together, four front.

Again the Japanese big guns and planes went to work, and again, as the rafts neared the island, the muzzles of guns appeared from among the rocks. But this time the guns in the rocks could not sweep the rafts clear, and so the Bean's battery opened up.

It was not until the rafts were almost up to the island that the Big Swords found out that they had been neatly tricked. There were no Japanese on them at all; only bayonets affixed to the timbers.

One of the planes, as the firing ceased, soared aloft and then did a few Immelman turns and side-slips, as if in derision. The Big Swords had wasted precious ammunition.

"Oi, vot suckairs ve are!" the Yid said. "Look at de ammunition ve haf vasted. Dem Japs is smart guys, ain't it?"

"Too damn smart for the likes ave ye!" Red answered. "Take a look at the ammunition we have left, ye Yid gibbon."

"Vot! For me? Didn't you shoot at de raft, too? You and all your section?—Didn't de Bean, und didn't George, und didn't—?"

The Bean came up. "Didn't you apes see that there were no Japs on board?" he asked sternly. "What do you mean by wasting ammunition like that? I've a darned good mind to court-martial both of you."

"Vot!—Und vot vas you didin'? Throwin' snowballs at dem? You vas higher dan us, und if you couldn't see, how could ve?"

"Do ye know what ye are, ye long-legged piece ave— Here comes George and Yang Chu."

"How much ammunition you got?" Grigsby asked the Bean.

"Enough to get tricked twice more, roughly speaking," answered the Boston Bean, gravely.

Grigsby smiled, then asked the Yid and Red the same question.

"Vell," answered the Yid, "I guess ve got it de same as de Bean—maybe three times more."

"Yeah? Well, we'd better try not to be tricked any more. Next time, we'll let them get right up to the shore. Place your guns on either side; the point is too steep for landing."

He walked away with the Manchu as indifferent to the steady rain of shells as was the Manchu noble.

THE NEXT RAFTS came down the same way, empty. They drew no fire.

Then down came still more rafts, this time loaded with Japanese.

And now the Big Swords saw something that made Red say, "Well, for the love ave all the good Saints! The banties have plenty ave sand in the craw ave them. Look at them little devils!"

As the rafts passed a point about five hundred yards up from the island, two Japanese regiments suddenly lined the banks, one on each side. Every man carried a bayo-neted rifle, officers and all. But each had his shoes off. As one man, while the rafts passed, they jumped into the river and began swimming towards the island.

"I've seen some brave things done," Grigsby said to Yang Chu, "and I think that this is one of the bravest. Swimming in ice-cold water, against machine guns. Too bad we have to do what we can to stop them."

The Manchu noble, whose ancestors had cut their way through countless Chinese to the Peacock Throne of China, looked at the swimming men. Their heads were bobbing up from bank to bank in a line thirty or forty feet thick. The Manchu's eyes were cold as he said:

"The mongrels of Nippon swim to meet their death from Manchu swords—as their ancestors walked to their death, a thousand years ago."

Grigsby, the Kentuckian, looked at Yang Chu for an instant. He knew that to the Manchu the brave Japanese infantrymen were no more than so many jackals which deserved to be slain.

"Line the shores with your men," Grigsby ordered.

The machine guns and rapid fire guns opened up on the rafts, and on the men in the water. No matter how any of the soldiers of fortune felt about Japanese bravery, or about the difficulty of shooting at swimming men, this was war, and the Japanese were now charging.

The Bean's battery, once he was sure that the figures on the rafts were not dummies, joined in. Not one of the rafts reached the island with a single Japanese soldier on his feet. Those of the swimmers that did succeed in landing met Manchu swords. All along the shore line, on both sides, there was fighting. The Japs, with their bayoneted rifles, fought to the end against the razor-sharp swords of the men of the House of Chi, who were bent upon avenging the deaths of the wife and family of the head of their house. The Japanese, of course, fought for Nippon, proud to die in her honor.

But they were outnumbered by the swordsmen; they were chilled by the icy waters; and they were fighting in their naked, slippery feet. And so at last, there were no more Japanese to kill. Many a Manchu, too, went on High with the Japanese.

RED AND THE Yid and the Bean watched the fighting on the left side of the island from a place high up under a rock.

"Vell," the Yid said, "give it dem credit.—Dey is scrappers. Did you see dot little guy vot climbed up on a rock und jumped down right in de middle of four swordsmen? Vot chance did he have? A bayonet against four swords. My, such a business!"

"Better go and pick out a nice sword, Mr. Cohen," the Boston Bean said. "Our boy friends are just getting started. Wait till they get warmed up. And our ammunition is about all gone."

"That's a good idea, Codfish," Red said. "I'll go get me wan so as to have it handy. What the hell do we care how warm they get? We'll chill 'em, wance they land, me bucko!"

"No doubt about it!" answered the Bean, politely. "At least so long as there is a single Dolan on his feet."

Red told the laughing Bean and the Yid where they could go, after doing certain things. The Bean, as soon as Red ran out of wind, said:

"Aside from that, of course, Mr. Dolan likes us, Mr. Cohen. That's his way of telling us how much he loves— They're at it again! *Adios, gents!*"

They were, as the Bean said "at it again." The Japanese did not seem to care how many men they lost. They were set upon taking the island, and that was that. This time there was no judging how many regiments entered the water after another lot of rafts had passed. The Japanese guns and planes kept up their frightful bombardment—

until some of the rafts would touch and the men on them, as well as the swimmers, gain a foothold on the island. Then, all of a sudden, the bombardment would cease.

Presently, the guns on the island became still. And a Japanese officer, watching through his glasses, smiled as he lowered them.

"They are out of ammunition," he announced. "We have them."

What he said about the ammunition was true; but he was wrong about the "we have them." The Japanese were far from having the Big Swords. Not by fifteen hundred-odd swords, wielded by Manchu swordsmen and others almost equal to the Manchus.

More and more Japanese arrived on the island, *via* the water and the rafts. But to collect and mop up an island like this one was a very hard thing to do, as the Japanese found out. It was bayonets against swords—swords on the rocks, beside the Japs in narrow places, and in places where one rock overlapped another. The Big Swords fought the Japanese to a standstill. Whenever one Big Sword went down, nevertheless, there was no one to take his place. On the other hand, whenever a Jap went down another stepped forward, and when he went down still another. The Japanese swarmed over the island as a hungry flock of sheep swarms over a green hillside. Not that the Japs resembled sheep. They were more like a swarm of angry hornets, lighting on the object of their wrath. And more hornets kept coming all the time.

RED AND THE Yid, armed with swords, fought beside the Cossack officers and the young Manchu Yang Chu, whose way of fighting with a sword had made a hit with Red.

As always, the Yid talked as he fought. "Come to poppa mit de pig sticker, little von!—Vot? Is dot the best you can do?" as his sword struck up a thrust. "Take dot, to learn it you somethink! I take it von of dem, Mistaire Cossack!—My, dot vos close! Take dis from Mistaire Cohen, for de honor of Hester Street!—Oi, von at a time, I esk you!" And so on....

As long as their ammunition held out and the Japanese they shot at went down, Grigsby and the Boston Bean fought with their Colt .45s.

But at last the Japanese won the island. Orders must have been given to take alive, if possible, any foreigners who were fighting with the Big Swords. The Japanese knew from the way the machine and rapid fire guns were operated that some of the soldiers of fortune must be on the island.

The Japanese evidently did not regard the Cossacks, the Russians and the Tartars as foreigners because they were ruthlessly slain. But first Red and the Yid, and then Grigsby and the Bean, were hammered into unconsciousness by rifle butts.

9

FROM THE OUTER DARKNESS

THE YID WOKE up slowly. Sitting up, he found that his head was sore, likewise his back and arms and ribs. But he grinned as he looked around the room in the island temple. Grigsby and the Boston Bean were sitting with their backs to the wall, and Red Dolan was lying on his back close to them.

"Vot de hell are you guys doing in the master's chamber? Is Red still mit?"

"He is," answered the Boston Bean, gingerly feeling his right forearm. "At the moment, Mr. Cohen, Mr. Dolan is taking a nap."

"My, dot vos some fight, ain't it! Dey saved us for something."

"Three guesses what."

"I only need it von! I bet you dot ve are to be taken to Tsitihar und turned over to de intelligence und de M.P. to play mit."

"Both Mr. Grigsby and I think that your guess is correct, Mr. Cohen. All the Japs have left these parts, except but one regiment."

"How you know dot, Beany?—My, I got a wallop on de sconce in the rear! Und my left side feels—!"

"Never mind itemizing, Mr. Cohen. We have a few assorted sore places ourselves. I know, because I watched the withdrawal from the slit over your head."

Red sat up. "What the hell now? Come on, let's slap 'em!—So they didn't kill ye, ye Yid monkey?"

"Not more dan eight or nine times, Irish bummer. As I went down I was hoping dot they got it you."

Red drew breath to answer, but Grigsby interrupted to say, "Let's cut that stuff for a little while. We are in a bad jam, and Jimmie will come right into it with us, unless the Japs move us out before he gets here. One of us has got to try to get away and warn him."

"I vill did it," answered the Fighting Yid, promptly. "Is dere a guard posted? If I could get to de river I could svim down it until I meet de T'aip'ing junks."

"That 'if' is a sad word," the Boston Bean answered. "Yes, my distinguished friend from Hester Street, *if* you could get to the river, you might swim down it. But take a look out that slit in the wall and count the Japs you can see. Start off with 'if I had wings.'"

"The only way to get out of this jam that I can think of," said Grigsby, "is for us to start a free-for-all fight among ourselves. The Japs will come in to stop it, and we can say that one of us has begun to weaken, and that we were merely starting to beat him to death for doing it. He might—"

"How do you mean, 'weakened,' George?" asked Red. "Talk plain, like Jimmie does."

"Why, Red, I mean that one of us—say the Boston Bean—suddenly announces to us that he is going to try and swap information about the Big Swords encampment, in exchange for his life.—The idea is that if we could arouse their suspicions sufficiently, maybe they'd take him out of here to save him from us. Then he might find a chance to escape."

" 'Tis an idea worthy ave Jimmie himself.—Go on, announce it, ye Bosting gibbon. I'll take the first crack at ye."

"All right. But listen, you gents. I'm sore all over right now. Don't make this scrap too realistic. The game is that—"

THE DOOR SUDDENLY opened, and two Japanese soldiers roughly pushed into the room a man whose head and face was bloody and whose coolie robes were torn and dirty. The man fell on his knees; then, as the door closed, he staggered to his feet. It was plain to be seen that he was about all in.

"Shih-kai!" shouted Red. "What the hell has happened to ye? Where is Jimmie?"

"Pipe down, Red," Grigsby said, as he started for Shih-kai. For a minute or so they tried to give Shih-kai first aid, but with neither water nor a first-aid kit, about all they could do was to bind up some of the cuts with bandages made from their own underwear and shirts.

At last Shih-kai held up his hand. "I have come back from the outer darkness, elder brothers. For a little while, at least. Captain Cordie is within three days of arriving here with ammunition—in the steamer Lao-Tzu. At Yungchoo, where the river turns to the east for many miles before it again turns west and north, I landed to come and tell you so that you might call in all raiding parties and hunting parties and be ready to unload. Captain Cordie wishes promptness in the—in the— A patrol of the mongrel of Nippon caught me and—I was brought here and tortured."

"You were tortured?" Grigsby asked. "They must know, then, that you are more than a Chinese coolie. Did any—?"

"Yes, elder brother, two of them did. As I was being brought in, along with other Chinese prisoners, a plane arrived from the south, bringing two officers. In passing, one of them looked over to where we stood, and his eyes lingered on me for a moment. Later I was brought before them. They knew that I was Shih-kai, of the T'aip'ing. I refused to tell them anything, and then—then they—I am tired, elder brothers, and would sleep."

His eyes closed; his head settled back in the crook of Grigsby's arm.

"May all the good saints protect Jimmie!" Red said, softly. "Into the trap is he comin', and us here wid no—"

"You're cuckoo, Mr. Dolan," the Bean interrupted. "The two officers may have known Shih-kai, but that does not mean that they know about Jimmie coming. They probably know that the T'aip'ing are backing the Big Swords, and have merely added Shih-kai to the bag to be taken to Tsitihar. They may pull out any minute now. A lot can happen in three days, old kid."

"He's breathing steadily," Grigsby said. "Make a pillow of your coat for him, Red."

10

STRANGE CLEVERNESS

A YOUNG JAPANESE lieutenant stood in front of several Japanese officers, among them Colonel Nagayo and Major Mito. The last two had flown up from Nienyeun. Word had come through the regular military channels that a large force of the Big Swords had been trapped at Chautin and was being destroyed by the Seventh Division. Hoping that some of the soldiers of fortune would be with the Big Swords—from whom, if not killed in action, information regarding the ammunition could be obtained—Colonel Nagayo had come up by plane, bringing with him Major Mito.

Up to the moment they left, no word had been received by any destroyer or plane that the Lao-Tzu had been sighted.

The reason for that was that the Lao-Tzu was well up the river, which was little traveled, and was running through desolate country. The planes and destroyers, as it happened, were hunting in the gulf, the ports, the inlets and the open sea. Colonel Nagayo hoped, by the use of a little third-degree technique, to learn where the ammunition was going to be landed. Then he would use the military radio. That the Seventh Division had, by chance, trapped the very detachment of Big Swords who awaited the ammunition never occurred to him. He figured that the destination of the ammunition must be some harbor of the Gulf of Fuchan, to the north. As a matter of fact, he did not know the course of the Fengning River.

As the young lieutenant finished speaking, Colonel Nagayo had hard work to keep his face impassive. Inside, his heart was singing with joy. He had thought that Shih-kai had come up with some news for the Big Swords about the ammunition, but the young officer had finished with:

"—as they made a pillow for the T'aip'ing called Shih-kai, I withdrew from the listening post."

He had repeated, word for word, all that had been said in the room at the temple where the prisoners were being held. It had been easy to make a hole in the wall, high up, while the Americans were still unconscious. This had been done before Shih-kai arrived, for the Japanese officers hoped that by posting there an officer who understood English, they might pick up the information as to where another body of Big Swords were.

The officer had related what was said from the time when the Yid first woke up. It was Colonel Nagayo who, as soon as he learned about the listening post, had stopped the torture of Shih-kai, and had had him put in with the soldiers of fortune, figuring that the Manchu, in his weakened and dazed condition, would do exactly as he had done.

One of the Japanese officers laughed. "And we were starting back to Tsitihar in the morning! Truly, we were disappointed at being sent back for replacements, but now—we are in at the death."

THE YID, DURING the time that the Jap officer was making his report, was looking out of first one slit and then another, on the three sides. And as if the Nine Red Gods were tired of playing on the Jap side, and had decided to back the soldiers of fortune for a little while, it happened that there was no Japanese with his ear to the hole at the moment when the Yid took his look-see.

"For the love ave Mike," Red said, "sit down, ye Yid chimpanzee. Ye make me nervous, walkin' around all the time. What the hell can ye see through them damn slits?"

"Vell, at least I don't have it to look at you, red-headt. I— Oi, dare is a Chink crawlin' over de rock—comin' dis vay."

During the Jap bombardment the old temple had been more or less knocked into a cocked hat; but it still stood, having been built of massive stone blocks. The nearest big rock was on the left, about thirty feet away. The top of the rock was about ten feet below the left slit.

"He is vounded," the Yid went on, "und— Dare he goes down in a crack! I vonder—"

"What the hell do you care about a wounded Chink?" demanded Red. "Ye chatter like a monkey-faced—"

"Here he comes again! My, he is huggin' de rock like a snake's belly. He is a Big Sword. I can tell by de jacket—von of Ying's men. Dot's de boy—don't slip off! Vot de hell is he—? He vants to talk to Shih-kai, I bet you!"

"What's that?" Grigsby asked, who had not been paying much attention to the Yid.

"Dare is a vounded Chink camin'. I bet he vants to talk to Shih-kai. Vake him up, George."

"See any Japanese close?"

"No. But dare are some vay down below. No place for dem to be on dis side, if dey ain't up on de rock mit de

Chink—und I can see all de top. Dot guy is a climber, no foolink!"

George Grigsby went over to where Shih-kai lay, his head on Red's coat.

"I am awake, elder brother," Shih-kai said, opening his eyes, "and I will get up and go to the slit as soon as the one who comes gets as close as he can. I now summon my strength back to me."

The Yid kept still for a minute, then he said, "He's come as far as he can, and he is lying dare looking at de slit."

Shih-kai rose without any help and went to the slit, the Yid giving way.

The others saw Shih-kai make some kind of a sign that brought his hand up to the side of his face. His back was turned to them, and that was all they could see. Then they heard his voice, very distinct, but not loud. They could not hear the answers of the Chinese on the rock, though Shih-kai spoke to him at length. After he had finished, he stood at the slit for three or four minutes, then turned to the soldiers of fortune.

"THE ONE WHO came is a little brother. He saw and recognized me as I was brought here. For a long time, his wounds would not permit him to move. But when the mongrels of Nippon drew away from where he was hiding, he struggled on to see if he could render assistance. I ordered that he try to escape from the island and go down the river, there to meet the Lao-Tzu and warn the black-eyed smiling one that the Nippon curs hold Chautin and the island, and that you, the war brothers of the black-eyed smiling one, are prisoners here."

"Ye did? Bully for ye, and for the little brother ave ye!" Red shouted. "Do ye think he will make it, Shih-kai?"

"He is badly wounded, O Lord of the Flaming Hair, and it may be that he will not have strength enough to withstand the cold of the river. I promised that if he succeeded, he and his relations to the ninth degree would be enriched and honored. I— My strength is departing from me.—The little men of Nippon may take him before he leaves the island, but that is as the gods will, Lord—"

Shih-kai pitched forward, to be caught and eased to the floor by the Yid.

"Wan hell ave a chance the Chink has, wid him wounded and all," Red proclaimed, bitterly. "The little Jap scuts are as thick out there as cold molasses in January. 'Tis to a deep, deep depth we have sunk when the life ave Jimmie depends on a wounded Chink! Sorry the—"

"Do we have to listen to that darned keening of yours any longer?" demanded the Bean. "Listen, old kid Dolan. Jimmie will go when his number goes up, and not before— just the same as you and I. What is the use of—?"

Red interrupted the Bean with, "Go to hell, ye Bosting—"

The door opened, and Colonel Nagayo, Major Mito and several other Japanese officers walked in, followed by a file of infantrymen.

"I trust," Colonel Nagayo said, as the soldiers of fortune rose to their feet, "that I am not interrupting an important conference, gentlemen?" His voice had the contented purr of a cat who sees a saucer of cream put down on the floor.

The Bean snapped into the play outlined by Grigsby. "I am glad you came"—he looked at the insigne on Nagayo's tunic and added—"colonel. These dirty bums were about ready to gang up on me. I told them that I was going to try and trade information about the Big Swords for my life, and they—"

One of the officers laughed. "The one who speaks is the Boston Bean," he announced in English.

Most Japanese officers speak and read English. Colonel Nagayo also spoke in English.

THE REST OF the officers joined in the laughter, and then Nagayo said:

"You cannot, as you Yankees say, put it over, Bean. We know all about it—from the time when one of you suggested this plan to deceive us. So you—the famous Codfish Duke of Massachusetts—would like to turn informer? There is another saying in your country which is, 'Tell it to the Marines.' That is what I think you had much better do, Bean; tell it to the Marines. Your past reputation for honorable conduct is very much against you now. Another might turn informer, but you—never. We have your record from the time you served in the Foreign Legion, through the A.E.F., and up to this minute in China. However, we will give you credit for the try—Captain Winthrop."

"No, I mean it," said the Bean. "I am sick and tired of this—"

"Silence, American mongrel! We come to tell you that we know that Captain Cordie is due to arrive on the Lao-Tzu very shortly, so we ask for your help in arranging a surprise party for him. You will assist us, we are quite sure."

"We will, like hell!" yelled Red. "Assist ye to surprise

Jimmie? All ye pink-toed midgets are goofy; and ye are the most goofy ave all, if ye—"

Three or four of the Japanese officers tensed, and one of them started for Red, who crouched to receive him.

Nagayo snarled a command in Japanese, and the officer stepped back. Then Nagayo went on, in English:

"He will pay for that—when he reaches Tsitihar. That is Red Dolan who speaks. After we are through with him, he will be red—all over. We have heard much of your cleverness, gentlemen. And yet you make plans openly, and you listen to messages, in a room which is not sound proof. You do not even lower your voices. Truly, that is a strange kind of cleverness.—Ah, I see my old friend the Fighting Yid. Are you still a trader, Yid?"

The Japs had caught the Yid once before, in Tsitihar, but the others had rescued him.

"Ven I get it a chance," answered the Yid, with a grin. "Vhy? Hev you got it somethink you want to trade?" The Yid had posed as a trader.

"Why—yes. I will trade you a look at the Lao-Tzu being taken for—let me see—your clothes.—Take off your clothes down to your underwear, all of you." The last was snarled out.

"Come and take the clothes off me, banty," Red snarled back. "It will take more than the likes ave ye to—"

"Why take another beating, Red?" Grigsby asked, calmly. "We haven't a chance. Do as the colonel orders. Tomorrow is another day, old kid."

"That is a very wise suggestion," Nagayo said, a smile on his lips. "You are—?"

"George Grigsby."

"The famous Major Grigsby of whom we have heard so much. Look, Major Mito. The famous soldier of fortune, Major Grigsby, is now stripping himself to his underwear, just to please us."

"It vould be a hell of a joke on dem if George didn't vare any!" the Yid said, as he took off his pants.

"What a di-ert-ty slur on all the Grigsbys of Kentuk'?" the Bean answered, as he took off his shoes. "Why, all the Grigsbys wear underwear, me good man."

A YOUNG JAPANESE officer who understood English whispered to the officer next to him. "Truly, what I have heard about them is correct. None of them have the least fear."

"Wait until Colonel Nagayo gets at them with the intelligence and the M.P. in Tsitihar. They will cringe and beg then."

When the prisoners had their clothes off, Colonel Nagayo motioned for two of the soldiers to pick up the garments.

"Watch for the Lao-Tzu," the colonel said, as the officers left the room, followed by the soldiers. "And see the surprise party we now go to arrange for them. It may be that Captain Cordie will insist that he join you here—if he remains in good health after the party is over."

"You know," the Bean said pensively, after the door had closed, "something tells me that I will never learn to like the colonel."

"George, what was he wah-wahin' about? Is there a—? Holy cats! He meant that somewan has been listening to us through a hole in the wall!"

"That's it, Red! And none of us thought of that possibility. His remark about our cleverness being a strange sort is correct, I reckon."

"I never did know dot de Japs vas a bunch of kidders before," the Yid said. "Vot a time dey vos having—mit us as de goats!"

"What now, George?" demanded Red.

"Well, all I can think of at the moment, Red, is for all of us to offer up a few prayers that Shih-kai's little brother gets to Jimmie in time for Jimmie to turn back. If they had a listening post, they may also have heard what Shih-kai ordered the wounded Chinese to do and—"

"Don't say it, George, darlin'! Don't even think it. 'Tis bad luck to put—"

"Vot do de Dolans know about luck—good or bad?" asked the Yid blandly.

11

THE WATCHERS

THREE DAYS PASSED, long days for the men in the room. Red Dolan was like a caged tiger. He couldn't keep still a minute, and he couldn't sleep. The Yid and the Bean did the best they could to occupy his attention, by making what Red termed dirty cracks about all the Dolans, and the one present in particular. But Red couldn't be switched off for more than a few minutes at a time.

Grigsby would explain patiently that there were many things that might happen to warn Jimmie of the trap; such as the chance that the Chinese might get through, that Jimmie might get word from the river junks that the Japanese were in force up near Chautin, or that bodies might float downstream far enough to tip Jimmie off to the fact that there was fighting up the river—and so on.

Red listened, agreed—and then began once more to walk around the room and to look downriver, through one of the slits. He set to retelling of the old days when Jimmie, the Bean, Grigsby and himself were in the Legion.

The others patiently babied Red along, knowing how he felt about Jimmie Cordie. The waiting was hard for them also, but for Red it was just plain hell, and they knew it.

Twice a day they were fed the regular Japanese ration, and water was left in the room.

On the morning of the fourth day, the Yid, who was looking out through the slit to the right, announced:

"Here comes it some rafts mit—von, two—maybeso three companies. Something is didink. *Oi,* I bet you de Lao-Tzu is caming."

Red jumped to the other slit, commanding the pier side of the island, and Grigsby and the Bean went to the remaining two slits. There was no activity, however, on the side Grigsby and Bean looked out on. From the Yid's slit, and from Red's, one could see the side of the island and down the river as well.

The Bean and Grigsby sat down again. "You will have to be an announcer, Mr. Cohen. You also, Mr. Dolan. One at a time, please."

"De Japs have landed, und de gang dot is here is meetin' dem. My, vot vould I give for just von Browning! I could make it dem hard to catch, und—"

"Never mind what you could do. Confine yourself to what *they* are doing, me good man," the Bean ordered.

"Mary Mother!" Red said. "They are goin' to try to decoy Jimmie to the island, instead ave takin' the ship at— Look at that, will ye? The di-ert-ty little monkeys. The curse ave Cru'mel on them for profanin' the dead that way."

"We would like to look," the Bean drawled. "But at the moment, what are they doing?"

"OI! THEY GOT it a lot of dead Big Swords propped up all around, stickin' mit de head and shoulders over de rocks, und dey are taking all de bodies on the shore, und hidin' dem. I vonder how dey expect to get avay mit it?"

"See that, Yid?" demanded Red. "Over there near the damn wharf? Wid our—"

"George and I will snatch you gents away from those slits, if you can't do better than that," the Bean said, firmly. "You see what, you red-headed ape?"

"See what, is it? I see this: up on small rocks placed behind some that is a little bigger stand four ave the little banties, wid our clothes on."

"What! Holy mackinaw! How the heck can they look like anything with our clothes on? Any of our tunics would make an overcoat for—"

"My, dot's clever!" the Yid interrupted. "Dey stand it on stilts. I can see dem from here. Und it looks like dare is a framevork all around dem, to hold it de coat. From a distance dey must look it like us. I vonder if dey is going to vave it signal flags or—"

"They probably don't know the Big Sword signals, Yid," Grigsby answered, calmly. "But the Jap buglers can imitate a Big Sword bugle without any trouble. Any call would attract the attention of the men on the bridge of the steamer, even if they didn't see the Big Swords—and us—on the rock. If Jimmie comes up the middle of the river, he can see, all right. That is what they figure. He will see and turn in. And if he keeps on going past, they have some way of signaling."

"See any artillery, Yid?" asked the Bean.

"No. None come over mit de push dot just arrived. Dare are four machine guns dot I can see from here. Dey vos already here."

"They think the steamer will be duck soup," Grigsby

said. "And it will be at that, once Jimmie and the T'aip'ing he has with him are—"

"Don't say it!" Red begged. "Don't ye do it, George Grigsby! Jimmie is too smart for them little—Mary Mother—all this means that the Chink didn't get through. They know she's comin'. They're settin' a trap—"

"So we imagine, from the preparations," the Bean answered. "Easy does it, Red. Remember that the Jap colonel said that Jimmie would be here with us. That means that he is going to be taken alive. It's a long way from here to Tsitihar, old kid. We've escaped before."

"Jimmie will fight them and—I have a warnin'. One ave them premon—predom— Never mind, I have a warnin'. Jimmie will fight to the death ave him on the deck ave the boat.—And us lookin' on, widout the power to—"

"Oi! I see it de colonel und de major and de rest of de guys vot kidded us. My, I hope dot dey board it de steamer und Jimmie gets his gun on dem. Dey vill do de rest of dare kiddink in hell. Dey are— Here she comes!"

Red began to talk to Jimmie. "Jimmie! Jimmie! Go by! Go by, Jimmie, darlin'. 'Tis a trap, Jimmie!—Go by, Jimmie!" As a man in the grandstand talks to the jockey of the horse he has bet on—when the jock is three-quarters of a mile away from him.

The Fighting Yid suddenly left the slit; and what he did proved that he was a gentleman as well as a scrapper. He said to Grigsby and the Bean, without a trace of the dialect he ordinarily used:

"Both of you fought in the Foreign Legion with Jimmie Cordie, and both of you are closer to him than I am. The slit is at your disposal."

"Thank you, Abie!" Grigsby answered, quietly. "Bean, you take it."

"I'm not having any. You take it. You and Jimmie have always—"

"I am now speaking as Major Grigsby. Take the slit, Captain Winthrop, and report what action you see."

"As you order, major," the Bean answered, saluting.

12

THE VICTORY

THE LAO-TZU CAME slowly up the river, and it seemed a million years to the men in the room before her bow came level with the island. She was, if anything, a little over towards the island from the middle of the river. The Lao-Tzu was an unknown steamer, looking a good deal like any of the big tramp steamers seen in Asiatic waters. She came past the pier, and then, as if her captain had accurately judged the current, turned and came in.

Red had gone from the heights to the depths. At first, when it had looked as if the Lao-Tzu would sail on past the island he had yelled, "Jimmie is on to them, the scuts! He's going past!—I knew it! I knew it all the time!" Then, as he saw that he had been mistaken, "He's—Mary Mother! The bow—turns towards us. They got Jimmie! They—got him!"

The Bean spoke like a radio announcer. Calmly, he described everything in sight. The Lao-Tzu was put alongside the pier by her captain, who knew Chinese rivers and the currents. Sailors jumped to the pier, ropes were tossed down and secured, the gangplank was run out, and the sailors scuttled up it to the ship.

"Can't Jimmie see that it ain't us?" Red shouted. "Jimmie,

ye blind man! The Big Swords are dead! That ain't us! Look out— E-e-e-e-e-eyah! Watch out!"

A company of Japanese infantry had come from behind the rocks and started down the pier at the double. When they got half way, however, the superstructure of the Lao-Tzu fell away and the muzzles of machine and rapid fire guns appeared. From the muzzles there came a rain of steel that cleared the pier of Japanese inside of two minutes; cleared it of all men on their feet, leaving dead and wounded men only.

The Boston Bean, who was not supposed to have any nerves, had hard work in keeping the pose of a calm, disinterested announcer. "Here comes Jimmie, with the T'aip'ing swords right behind," he said. "About one hundred and fifty of them. It looks as if the guns were trying to erect a fence on either side.—Here comes another Jap company, with bayonets fixed. From both sides.—They're crouching and coming through the fence.—A lot of them are down.— The rest make it, and are tying into the T'aip'ing.—Holy cats! What a fight. I can't see Jimmie, though. He's in the thick of it."

A LITTLE LATER—TWO or three minutes—the Bean announced, "T'aip'ing swords have won, gents. Here they come, Jimmie and two swordsmen leading. Jimmie looks as if he were wounded in the left arm.—I wonder why the Japs didn't lay off and use their rifles? They could have bushwacked the whole gang from the top of—"

"Probably they thought they were better men with bayonets than the T'aip'ing were with swords," Grigsby answered.

Said the Yid, "You said it to confine yourself to what

they are doing. Do it, den, Codfisher. It's a poor rule dot don't work both vays. Never mind vy de Japs charged mit bayonets!"

"Oh, yeah?—Here comes a couple of platoons from the right, and—two machine guns on top of a rock. The machine guns open, and—that's knocking 'em off the Christmas tree, old kid!—Pardon me, gents. Some gunner on the Lao-Tzu caught the machine gun crews from flue to flitter, with two bursts."

The gunner on the ship was Carewe, who had insisted that he was now well enough to operate a gun. He proved it, for the machine gun crews were slain to the last man.

"Some of the Japs get through and—Jimmie's down!—He's getting up.—No, there he goes down again. Two of the T'aip'ing get to him and are holding off three Japs. Here comes more T'aip'ing—Jimmie's up! The platoons are no more.—Not such a heck of a lot of T'aip'ing left, either. The Japs are fighting like darn good and mad wildcats.—Here they come once more, and—that will be all.—No can see from slit, now. It's a case of up and over and under and around rocks."

"Jimmie will slap 'em to hell outta the way," Red said, as he left his slit. He couldn't see any longer, either. Red had been talking to Jimmie all the time, though Jimmie was at least a thousand yards away.

"Come on, Jimmie!" Red had yelled, half mad with excitement. "Come on, ye half-pint size ave nawthin'! Quit that damn high parryin', ye scut!"

Jimmie had emptied his Colt, and as there was no time to reload, had picked up a T'aip'ing sword.

"Lower! Lower!—Look out for that little devil sneakin'

up from—I thought he had ye that time! Don't take two ave them on at wance, that way!—That's smackin 'em, Jimmie. Come on, ye black-muzzled shrimp."

On the island, when the fight started, there had been roughly four hundred Japanese, counting the two companies which the Yid had seen arriving. Not that it had been thought that four hundred were needed to take a tramp steamer, for most of them had been set to hunting among the rocks for Japanese dead and wounded. The machine gun section was there to salvage the Big Swords' guns. The Japs did not want the guns for themselves, but they would make a very much appreciated present for some friendly war lord or general. One company was more than sufficient to take the steamer—or would have been under ordinary circumstances.

WHEN THE STEAMER arrived, the Japanese had been more or less scattered over the island, except for the company which was detailed to take the steamer, and the other company that had charged. Why the Japanese did not do as the Bean said, and use their rifles from ambush, could not be figured out. Possibly, as Grigsby said, they thought they were better men than the T'aip'ing. Whatever the reason, they charged from wherever they reached the rescue column; sometimes eight or ten of them, at other times more, and several times two or three, Japs would jump down from rocks in front of the T'aip'ing and die there, trying to stop the advance.

The guns from the ship ceased firing just as the Bean said that he couldn't see any more. They were forced to, for the column had swung to the right to clear a rock.

Two more machine guns were carried up on a rock by

the Japs and put in action—for a minute or so only. Twenty of the T'aip'ing went up the rock like cats climbing a tree. When they came back there were only six of them. There were no more Japanese machine gunners, however.

The little Japanese infantrymen, collectively and individually, gave the T'aip'ing swords all the fight they wanted—and if it had not been for the fact that one company had been destroyed at the pier, and another shortly afterwards, there can be no question that Jimmie Cordie and the T'aip'ing would never have reached the temple. Officers and men of the Japanese attacked, fought like madmen—and died.

The Yid had gone to the slit abandoned by the Boston Bean and was looking at the Lao-Tzu. Suddenly he said:

"*Oi*, here dey come! Mit Jimmie in de lead! Dare is only a few of dem left, und Jimmie's face und head und right shoulder is bloody. Und his left arm is out of commission. Dare are about— Here comes it some more Japs around de corner of a rock. Two officers und six or seven men.—My, such scrappers dey are. Von of dem—dey are de colonel und de major vot kidded us! I bet you dey vaited up here to get a crack at de finish ven de— Oi, dot vas close!"

Colonel Nagayo and Major Mito had not charged with the second company, nor had they joined any other group that charged. They were intelligence officers, and it was not their business to fight side by side with infantrymen.

The two officers had gone almost to the temple, after seeing that the infantry was attacking without waiting to form a line of battle. As a matter of fact, a line of battle could not be formed on the island because of the rocks, and if the Japs had waited to get their men together in order to try to hold the winding, twisting way to the temple, the rescue column would have been there and gone before the Japs could accomplish their purpose.

As it was, Colonel Nagayo stopped what men he met, hoping to collect more and to hold the temple—intelligence officer or no intelligence officer—until reinforcements came from the mainland. But the column moved too fast for him to do so, and as the column turned the last rock in the way and started up the temple path, the two Jap officers charged, with the men they had.

As he closed in, Colonel Nagayo fired at Jimmie Cordie with his service revolver. That was one of the few shots fired, outside of the machine guns. The Jap officers had gone in with bayoneted rifles, the same as their men.

The bullet left a red streak on Jimmie's neck, just under his left ear. As Jimmie cut at Nagayo, someone pushed the colonel a little to one side, and Jimmie missed him. But, backhanded, Jimmie sent the heavy sword hilt crashing into Nagayo's face. The Japanese colonel went down like a poled ox.

Major Mito was killed by a T'aip'ing.

There was a swirl of fighting men, and then—Jimmie Cordie and some of the T'aip'ing ran into the temple.

HALF A MINUTE later, the door of the room opened and Jimmie Cordie stepped in. He was more or less covered with blood—his own and that of the Japanese—and his left arm hung lifeless by his side. There was a wound in his right shoulder, and blood was coming from the graze in the neck. But his eyes were bright and smiling as ever and there was a grin on his lips.

"I hate to bust up your party," he said, "but the excursion boat is due back at Pier 38 in—"

"Jimmie! Ye made it! Ye made it, ye scut ave all creation!— And we thinkin' that the Chink didn't get through."

"He did, though. I took time out to mount a few trinkets on the Lao-Tzu, and to teach the T'aip'ing how to— Are you all right, Shih-kai?" Jimmie asked hastily.

"Yes, honorable elder brother. My heart is singing with joy that you are here."

"So is mine, war brother, now that I see you. Can you walk?"

"Yes—but slowly, I am afraid."

"Carry Shih-kai, Red. Come on, you apes. No telling how many Japs are on the mainland."

"Jimmie, did ye—?"

"Tell you all about it on the boat.—Let's go! There may be a lot more Japs here to play with."

But there were no more Japs on the island to play with— that is, no more unwounded Japs.

"Jimmie, vill I carry it you?" asked the Yid.

"No, thanks. I can make it. If I fall down, pick me up, Abie. We've got to get the T'aip'ing wounded."

On the way down from the temple they passed Colonel Nagayo, who was now sitting up. His face was a mess, though he could still see. As Jimmie reached him, the colonel tried to pick up his revolver, which had fallen a little away from him.

Jimmie kicked the weapon still further away. "It is all over—colonel. Take it easy until your medical corps gets here. You can try for me some other day."

"You are—Captain Cordie?" asked Nagayo, through cut and swollen lips.

"Yes, I am Captain Cordie."

"I am—Colonel Nagayo. As you say, I can try for you—some other day."

"Help yourself to the mustard," Jimmie answered, as he walked on toward his men.

THE LAO-TZU PULLED away from the pier with all the T'aip'ing wounded on board. She was opposite the timber when the rest of the Japanese regiment shoved off on rafts. The Japs knew that they had no chance of taking the steamer, even if they succeeded in putting their rafts alongside. And so, as a machine gun opened on them, trained high on Jimmie's orders, the Japs jumped from the rafts and swam ashore. Whether that ought to be described as a retreat or merely one of those rearward movements is difficult to say.

The Lao-Tzu proceeded north towards a village where Jimmie knew that the ammunition could be landed. Incidentally all reached the Big Sword headquarters.

The Yid, standing in the stern of the Lao-Tzu, made a gesture that took his thumb and the tip of his nose; a gesture directed toward the Japs, some of whom had managed to reach shore. He hoped they could see that gesture.

A little later, Red joined him. "The doc says that Jimmie will be all right, save for a scar on the neck. Carewe is all right, and Shih-kai will be, damn soon. Laugh that off, ye Yid beneath notice!"

"Dare is somethink else I rather laugh at," answered the

Yid blandly. "Pardon me vile I laugh it up my sleeve for five minutes, Mistaire Dolan."

"What the hell have ye to laugh at now?" demanded Red.

"At the varnin' you got. Never speak it to me again about varnin's, Irish loafer. You had it de varnin' dot Jimmie would fight it to de death on de deck of de boat, mit us looking on. Phooy on you und your varnin's! Get it von now about—"

"Well—ye Yid scut! Here I come, all happy and joyful about Jimmie, and yet— Ye hook-nosed ape ave the world, ye start trouble! For wan cent I'd...."

At some length Red told the Yid what he would do for a cent, and after he had finished the Yid started him all over again by saying, "My! All dot for a cent? And vot would it you do for a dollar, Irish *gonif?*"

THE WHITE WAR LORDS

Jimmie Cordie and his soldiers of fortune, on a rescue mission, did not know about that Japanese trap

1

INTO DANGER

A STRONG COLUMN of the Big Swords rode towards the foothills of the mountains of northwest Manchukuo.

They were on their way to the Big Sword headquarters in the hills after, as one of the Manchu officers said, "lessoning" the Japanese in regards to leaving only two regiments to guard an important railroad center.

With the column rode five Americans and one Englishman, six of the most famous soldiers of fortune in the Orient. The Big Swords, as far as the riders went, wore no special uniform. The infantry regiments and the artillery wore uniforms but the Manchu swordsmen and the men of other races who made up the cavalry wore about what they pleased to protect themselves from the cold of the hills. All the Manchus wore, under their outer robes, the silk, sleeveless fighting shirt of the Manchu swordsman. When they charged they discarded the robes.

The soldiers of fortune all wore heavy leather riding trousers, leather tunics, fur and leather caps with ear muffs and high laced boots of split cowhide. Around their waists were cartridge belts from which hung holstered .45 Colt revolvers, and all wore shoulder belts full of .30-30 Winchester cartridges.

The rifles were carried in sheaths hooked to the saddles. They were all lean, hard-bitten men with weatherbeaten faces and calm, cold eyes.

Captain James Cordie, ex-Foreign Legion sergeant and captain of machine gun company, A.E.F., slim, wiry, black eyed and tight lipped; second in command of all Big Swords, rode at the head of the column with two of the Manchu nobles of the House of Chi.

"I think we had better make it to the river, Tseng," he said, "and hole up there for a week. The wounded can't stand the trip through the pass of the lower mountain the way they are."

"I think so also, honorable elder brother. A week at the river will make them once more well and strong." They spoke in Pushtu, the universal language of the border.

"All right, we'll give them the week."

The advance patrols were called in and the column turned left towards the river Kokong.

The Jap stared, then drew their revolvers.

"What the hell now?" demanded a big, red-headed man riding with the machine gun section. "What are we turnin' left for? 'Tis not the way to the pass." He was Red Dolan, ex-Foreign Legion and lieutenant of military police, A.E.F. No matter where Jimmie Cordie was one did not have to look far to find Red Dolan.

A man riding beside Red, who looked to be about as broad as he was long, with an unmistakable Semitic face, answered, "Dere is a drug store down on de corner. Maybeso Jimmie has got it de headache und vants to get a powder. Vot do you care, Irish bummer?"

He was the famous Fighting Yid, Jimmie Cordie's first sergeant in France. The Yid's real name was Abraham Cohen, born on Hester Street, New York City, but few people knew it.

"What? I asked ye a civil question, didn't I, ye Yid scut? And how do ye answer me? Ye answered me wid scorn and contempt, ye cross between a monkey-faced gibbon and a

Gone was the
Afghan disguise.

black and white kitty. Sorry the day Jimmie ever detailed the likes av ye wid a Dolan."

"A Dolan," answered the Yid with a smirk, "should be proud to be detailed mit a Cohen. De Cohens alvays took it care of de Dolans. Vonce, vay back in de dim past, dare vas a Cohen who vos a king in—"

"A king? A Cohen a king? Listen to me, ye beneath notice, flat faced duck av a Hester Street—"

A tall, lanky, sorrowful faced man crowded his horse between the horses of Red and the Yid. "Gimme room. Gangway for a berth deck cook and third admiral of the Swiss navy. Why the turn to the left?" He was the Boston Bean, ex-Foreign Legion and captain of artillery, A.E.F.

"An' what the hell business is it av yours?" demanded Red, promptly. "If ye must know, ye Bosting codfish, there is a drug store down on the corner and Jimmie has the headache. We're goin' down there to get him a powder. Now ye know all about it."

The Boston Bean, down in the Massachusetts Social Register as John Cabot Winthrop, sighed deeply. "It certainly is hell and high water that a perfect gentleman like myself has to put up with the gutter sweepings of Cork. I ask a—"

"Dot is just vot I vos sayin', Beany," interrupted the Yid. "I started to tell it dis Irisher about de Cohens und de—"

"The both av ye," Red said as he tightened his reins, "can go to hell wid my compliments. I'm goin' up wid Jimmie."

The column reached the river and made camp. There were quite a few wounded and it took a little time to make them comfortable. The second day, Jimmie Cordie walked over to where Red, the Bean and the Yid were sitting in the shade of a tree at the river bank.

"I'm going to make a little social call," he said. "Want to go along, Yid?"

"Sure do I, Jimmie. Who ve going to call on?"

"I'll go wid ye, Jimmie darlin'," Red said. "What the hell is the idea av takin' this Yid monkey callin'? He don't know how to act wid roughnecks, let alone anywhere else. I'll go wid ye."

"Better leave both Mr. Dolan and Mr. Cohen at home, Jeems, me good man," the Boston Bean put in. "I'll go with you to maintain the honor of the family, if there weren't ham the Yid would probably raise chain lightning and Red—the good Lord knows what he would do—eat his pie with a knife and think the—"

"Oh, I would, would I? Well, listen to me, ye long legged cross between a jack-snipe and a—"

Jimmie Cordie laughed. "I'd take a chance with either one of them, Beaneater, but at the moment I'm going to take the Yid. You are in charge of the wounded and Red has got to keep still for a few days with that leg of his. How is it, Terence Aloysius?"

"Aw, hell, the leg av me is all right. 'Tis only a scratch, Jimmie. I'll go wid ye."

"You will not. I'm going over and see Changchau. His city is up the river about thirty miles. It's the first chance I've had to drop in and say 'How.' Come on, Yid."

"Jimmie, is he the lad that was in Tonkin the time we was there?"

"Yeah. He fought for old General Kai-shi-Lung, remember?"

"I do—an' a game little banty he is. Are ye takin' enough av an escort, ye reckless shrimp av the world?"

"I'm takin' the Yid. He's enough escort, isn't he?"

"That scut av the world? He is not. Wan Dolan is worth twenty-wan Yids like him any time."

"Oi, says it you, dot's all. Says it you. Von Cohen can—"

"Go on, Yid, get ready. Never mind about the Cohens and the Dolans. Red, you let the Bean attend to that leg while I'm gone. You hear me?"

THE CITY OF the War Lord Changchau was not a large one, but it was walled in a strategic place on the river and therefore easy to defend.

Changchau was a young man and took more chances than an older man would. He opened his city to all kinds of caravans, coming and going from the hills, so that his people could make some money selling supplies and what not. Most war lords only opened their gates to those they knew and were sure of, but Changchau opened his gates to all traders. He was confident that his rifle regiments and battery could shoot any out of his city that he did not want in it.

He welcomed Jimmie Cordie and the Fighting Yid and the small escort of Big Swords that came with them, some thirty-five men, with open arms. He had been in a more than tight place down in Tonkin where it looked very much as if his ancestors on high were going to have a chance to welcome him to his reserved seat among them. Jimmie Cordie had gone in with a machine gun and saved Changchau's bacon. The young Chinese fighting man never forgot it, and when Jimmie dismounted he literally fell on Jimmie's neck and kissed his collar.

The honor guard paraded through the city, Changchau riding between Jimmie and the Yid towards the palace.

As the parade passed an inn, several of the men who had come in with a caravan were sitting around outside. For the most part they were Kirghiz tribesmen, the real thing. But two of the men who watched the parade, although as dirty and hairy looking as the others, and dressed in equally sloppy sheepskins and various skin rags, were far from being Kirghiz. They were Major Shima and Captain Noto of the Japanese Military Intelligence who had been on the eastern slope of the mountains, in Red territory, to find out what they could about Red massing of troops.

"Look—it is Captain Cordie and the Fighting Yid of the Big Swords!" Major Shima said softly. "If we could only kill them both here in the city of Changchau, Colonel Nagayo would see to it that we both were stepped up—maybe to colonels."

"I see them. But—how could we, major? We are lucky to be this far on our way to headquarters. I know that the colonel would give much if the men who flouted him were—"

"Ease back, Captain Noto, towards that little shack. We will try and plan. It may be that we can send both of the mongrels to the outer darkness. Once we have done so, we can get away from the city easily enough and leave the Kirghiz to, shall I say, explain matters to this young fool who thinks he is a war lord."

JIMMIE CORDIE AND the Yid were wined and dined by Changchau and invited to listen to the singing girls and watch the dancers. The standing of Changchau was greatly enhanced among his officers and men by the presence

as friends of the two famous soldiers of fortune who led
the Big Swords and he made the most of it. Not that he
wouldn't have given Jimmie Cordie anything he had, but if
his officers and men knew that he had close relations with
the powerful, dreaded Big Swords, why, that was quite all
right also.

At last, before Changchau could call for the singers and
dancers, Jimmie Cordie called a halt.

"No, little brother. We have ridden hard all day and are
very tired. You have filled us with food and drink. Now we
would sleep, knowing that we sleep in safety, surrounded
by your rifles."

Changchau promptly agreed, and escorted Jimmie and
the Yid to the stone house close to the palace where the
Big Sword escort was already settled down for the night.
The Big Swords had picketed their horses on the right side
of the house and were sitting around camp fires as Jimmie
and the Yid came up.

Jimmie, who drank very little, had turned his glass upside
down early in the evening. The Yid, who liked his liquor,
had kept his glass right side up, and as a result, while he
knew what it was all about, was very close to being "three
sheets in the wind."

"My, dis is a svell place, ain't it, Jimmie?" he asked, as he
and Jimmie stepped into the room on the ground floor
that Changchau had ordered made ready for his distinguished guests.

"Yeah, boy. Take that couch over there, Yid. Chinese
hospitality leaves nothing to be desired, does it?"

"Vell, I vould have liked to have seen it de dancing girls
und listened to de—"

Jimmie laughed. "You've seen, and heard, and had plenty, Mister Cohen. Get to bed. We've got some riding to do in the morning."

"Oi, vot do ve have to go back so soon for? Changchau tells it me dot in de morning he vill break out some of dot Fu-kan brandy for my special benefit. Maybeso ve stay a little vile, ain't it?"

"And maybeso we don't, old kid. Go to sleep, and if you snore, there will be a new face in the Yid angel chorus by morning."

THE TWO JAPANESE intelligence officers sat with an old Chinese woman in a house not far from the inn. A few, seemingly indifferent questions put to one of the girls at the inn had brought out the fact that the old woman and her family of children and grandchildren had lived in the stone house where the "foreign devils" were now quartered. The Lord Changchau, on his arrival from the south, had said that the family was too near the palace and so had moved them.

Both Japanese officers could speak Chinese, and after feeling their way, had put a few silver coins in the old woman's hand. To her, the coins meant that during the winter she could have many luxuries that she had longed for, but had never been able to attain. They outweighed any loyalty she had to China or her war lord or anything else, for that matter. The Japanese intelligence officers very soon found that out, and once they did, told her that they were not Kirghiz but men of Nippon who had come to see to it that all poor people became rich and powerful, and so on.

The old woman did not care whether they were men of Nippon or men of the moon; she had coins in her hand.

"Say what you wish me to do," she snarled. "Do not beat around the bush so much. Tell me, and if I can do it, will there be more coins?"

"This then, old mother of many sons. The men of the Lord Changchau who now guard the stone house, do they know you?"

"That I do not know until I see them. I have lived here always, and most of the men who fight for the Lord Changchau know me. It may be that some of the men he brought with him from the south do not."

"It is not far from here. Will you go and see if you know the officer of the guard or any of them?"

"Yes, I will go. Wait here for me."

Not more than ten minutes later the old woman was back. "Yes, I know the officer, and also the men under him. He is Kai Lu, whom I have known since he was born. What now?"

"This, venerable one. Have you any clothes belonging to your sons or grandsons that will fit us?"

The old woman looked at the two Japanese for a moment, then answered, "Yes, I have clothes that will fit you. What of it?"

"Have you also four of your sons or grandsons within call? I mean those who are now men?"

"Yes, four or twice that many."

"Will they obey you without question?"

"Yes."

"If you, with six of your sons and grandsons, came up to the officer of the guard and told him that you had come to remove some foodstuffs that you had stored in the cellar of the house, would he believe you and let you in the house?"

"Yes, Kai Lu would believe me and let me in to get the foodstuffs—but there is no food there, and when we came out, empty handed, what then?"

Major Shima smiled. "Truly you are clever, mother of great fighting men and students."

As a matter of fact he had not figured further than the getting in of Captain Noto and himself and their getting out by themselves after driving knives into the hearts of Captain Cordie and the Fighting Yid. Whoever helped them get in was to get out the best way they could. And what happened to them afterwards was a matter of no concern to the Japanese.

Major Shima's brain was well trained, fast and clever, and there was hardly a pause between sentences as he kept on with, "Your six sons and grandsons will carry under their robes empty sacks. Once in the cellar the sacks can be filled with dirt. There is your food to bring out."

"But there are Manchu swordsmen sitting around camp fires close to the house. What of them?"

"They may come forward and ask the officer of the guard what you want. If they do he will tell them that you formerly lived in the house and wish to go in and get some foodstuffs left there. It is very simple, old mother. Why should not the Manchu swordsmen believe it?"

"I do not know. You are doing the planning, not I. If they believe and we go in, what then?"

"I will tell you. We wish to talk to the two foreign devils and offer them much money to join us in the fight we are making for the poor people. This we could not do openly, because if your war lord knew that we were not Kirghiz but men of Nippon we would be slain. He is for the rich and powerful people as we are for the poor and needy. We cannot go up to the foreign devils and tell them who we are as long as there are any Manchus or Chinese close enough to them to hear what we say. This way we can talk to them with safety."

The old woman grunted and opened her hand to look once more on the coins. "Cover my other hand also with coins and I will do as you wish. I take my sons and grandsons into danger and it is worth much more money. If the Lord Changchau finds out that through me you talked to the foreign devils, there will be much pain suffered by me and mine."

"This we will do," answered Major Shima. "We will cover your other hand now with coins and, if the matter goes smoothly, when we are back here we will cover both of them again."

"Cover it, then." The old woman opened her hand. "I will get clothes and call my sons and grandsons."

2

ASSASSINS

THE YID COULD not get to sleep. It may have been the liquor or it may have been the thought of what he was missing in regards to the singing and dancing girls, or both. Anyway, he could not sleep. Finally he sat up and looked over to where Jimmie Cordie lay on another couch.

"Jimmie, you avake?" the Yid asked softly. Getting no answer the Yid got up and walked over to a window. The moon was out and it was almost as light as day outside. In the room it was a little darker, but still light enough to see fairly well.

The Yid could see the embers of the camp fires and the Big Swords lying near, their saddles for pillows. There were no lights in the palace, at least on the side that the Yid could see. Everything looked peaceful and quiet.

"Dey take it de sidevalks in about ten o'clock in dis man's town," the Yid announced to the world in general. "I vish I knew it vare—dere is somevon sneaking up de hall."

The Yid had been noted on the Western Front for his more than acute hearing. It was claimed by his admirers that the Fighting Yid could hear a German blow his nose ten miles away on a stormy night, which was more or less of an exaggeration. Even so, there was no question that the Yid could hear better than most men.

He started over to wake Jimmie Cordie, moving as quickly as a big bear.

The plan formed by Major Shima had worked perfectly. A Manchu officer of the Big Swords had walked over as the old woman and her party reached the officer of the guard. The two Japs were in the middle, and with their heads capped and held as far down as possible without exciting comment, they passed readily as Chinese, because neither the officer of the guard nor the Manchu were at all suspicions.

The Chinese officer explained, "This old woman and her family used to live here and have come to get some food-stuffs stored in the cellar."

"Do not let them disturb the war lords who are sleeping," the Manchu answered as he turned away. "They should have come in the daytime."

"She says that she could not get her sons and grandsons then."

That sounded all right to the Manchu, as it had sounded to the Chinese officer.

The party, led by the old woman, went into the house through a shed in the rear.

The Yid touched Jimmie on the shoulder. "Jimmie, vake up. Ve are going to have it callers. Jimmie—vake up."

Like most men who live always in an atmosphere of danger, Jimmie Cordie was a light sleeper, and had the faculty of waking instantly with a clear brain. He was awake before the Yid started to talk. The touch on his shoulder did it.

He was on his feet beside the Yid as the Yid muttered the last "vake up."

Neither Jimmie nor the Yid had undressed. They had taken off their cartridge belts and put them at the head of the couches. They had no more idea of being subject to attack than they did that they were to make one. Even so, their .45 Colts in the holsters were within reach of their hands as they lay on the couches.

Now, the Yid was away from his couch, and Jimmie Cordie, the way the Yid was standing, could not, as he got to his feet, reach for his Colt.

As a matter of fact, he did not think of doing it. What he thought was that Changchau had sent some message or some liquor for the Yid, or that some Big Sword officer wanted to see him. There was not much time to think anything between the time he got on his feet and the opening of the door.

He and the Yid saw two men dressed in Chinese robes come softly into the room. Both men had daggers in their right hands. To Jimmie and the Yid they were two Chinese assassins who expected to find their prey fast asleep.

The room was lighter than the hall, and the two Japanese had to take a split second to get their eyes adjusted. That was long enough to enable the Yid to grab up one of the silken pillows Jimmie had been lying on, crouch and hurl himself straight at them. The pillow was to take the dagger thrust the Yid knew would come.

MAJOR SHIMA STEPPED forward to take the charge of the Yid, the dagger held as a sword. Captain Noto, his dagger held point down, rushed at Jimmie Cordie. They had both seen the two soldiers of fortune standing by the couch, and both knew that instead of quietly putting their daggers into the hearts of sleeping men, they had a fight on their hands. And this much can be said of the two Japs, they went right in.

The Yid swung at the dagger with the pillow while he was off his feet in the flying tackle. The pillow missed because Major Shima, who was pretty fast himself, lowered the dagger blade. In doing it, though, he had to bend his wrist downward and raise his elbow up. It was an awkward position to thrust from and with the Fighting Yid arriving full force, awkward positions were to be avoided.

The Jap major did get the dagger point up, and did start a thrust, but that was all he had time to do before the Yid's body hit him. The dagger point went between the Yid's right side and arm, and the edge cut through the heavy tough leather of the Yid's tunic and cut the Yid's side just enough to draw blood.

The next second Major Shima went down, the Yid on top of him and the Yid's right hand closed on the right wrist of Major Shima. "I got him, Jimmie! Lie still, Mistaire Knifeman, or poppa vill break it de— Oi! let it go de—"

Jimmie Cordie had enough to do on his own account without paying any attention to the Yid. As Captain Noto rushed him, Jimmie stepped away from the couch and started to circle with light, mincing steps. The Jap captain struck at him twice and missed both times. Most men who use a dagger know that if it is held as a sword is held there is that much more reach to it. But Captain Noto either did not know it or would rather use the downward stroke, longer reach or no longer reach.

As he raised the dagger for a third try, Jimmie Cordie

swayed in and his right fist flashed up in an uppercut. If it had landed, Captain Noto of the Japanese intelligence would have taken a rapid journey to the land of Nod. But it did not land. The little Jap captain was, as the Yid would say, "dare like a duck himself, ain't it?" He moved his head back the fraction of an inch and struck at Jimmie like a copperhead.

Jimmie Cordie, as he missed, turned a little and tried for a neck hold. He did not get it, and the dagger point went into his shoulder. Not as deep as Captain Noto intended, because Jimmie's turn swung the shoulder out an inch or so. But it went deep enough to tell Jimmie Cordie that he had better not miss again if he wanted to remain among the living. He brought his right knee up as hard as he could—and this time he did not miss.

Captain Noto groaned with anguish and the dagger fell from his hand.

Jimmie lunged against the would-be assassin and this time got a hold. Up to the moment he did not know that the man was anything but a Chinese. He did right after as his hold was broken and one clamped on him. That jujutsu hold told him that it was a Jap and another thing told him the same. Captain Noto snarled something in Japanese as his left hand began to press on Jimmies Adam's-apple.

The Yid and Major Shima were staging a messy fight over in one corner. The major had let go his knife, because the Yid's grip had stopped all blood from coming up in the major's right hand.

The blood that Jimmie was losing through the shoulder wound weakened him, and Captain Noto threw him off, then staggered to his feet. Jimmie lit on the side of the couch and fell over it.

As he did there came a shout from outside to the right, and a command was given. Another command was yelled from the front of the house.

Major Shima bit his lower lip until the blood spurted out, to withstand the pain of the Yid's hold, and with a superhuman effort put a hold on the Yid's neck that put the Yid out of commission.

The Jap major got to his feet. "The alarm! We will be taken here like rats in a trap! To the window, Captain Noto! See if the way—"

Captain Noto was at the window before the major finished the command. "The Big Swords run towards the rear and front! All of them! The way is clear, Major Shima. First will we do what we—"

The sound of running feet in the hall came clearly.

"No time! Quick! Outside! We try for the wall. If we can make the hills we—"

Captain Noto was out the window and Major Shima stopped talking and followed.

Jimmie Cordie got to his feet, his head swimming, and went around the couch after his gun. As he stopped for it the door opened and Big Swords crowded into the room. **"SAY WHAT IS** to be done to these degraded ones. To them and to all their relations to the ninth degree. Remembering before you pronounce sentence that they have brought unmerited disgrace upon me, your war brother."

Jimmie Cordie looked at the line of prisoners that stood in front of the stone house. Then he looked at the impassive face and eyes of Changchau. In the line there stood the old woman, her sons and grandsons and the Chinese officer of the guard, Kai Lu.

He knew that they could expect about as much mercy from Changchau as from a hungry tiger. That they had been fooled by the Japanese would make no difference. Then he looked at the Yid who stood beside him.

It was morning and Jimmie's shoulder had been treated and bandaged. The Yid was as ever with the exception of a very sore throat and ears that looked as if they had been rubbed with sandpaper.

"How about it, Yid?"

"Vot de hell are you putting it up to me for?" demanded the Yid. "Do I look it like a guy dot vants to see people boiled mit oil or skinned alive? Look at de relations back of de line."

Back of the line of prisoners there stood a terrified bunch of men, women and children.

Jimmie Cordie was in a bad box and he knew it. He knew that if he asked for mercy it would be construed as weakness on his part by Changchau and the Chinese and the Big Swords present, and that word would soon spread that "The Big Sword officers were as weak women. They ask for mercy towards those who try to slay them." And that impression was the last thing Jimmie Cordie wanted to be circulated. The fact that the Big Swords were dreaded for their ruthlessness kept many a bandit leader in his place. And yet—there were the gray faces and lips of the women and children who had committed no fault.

He looked at the line as if making up his mind just what form of torture to start off with—praying for an "out" at the same time. His eyes reached those of the Chinese officer, Kai Lu, and the out came to him. There was something about Kai Lu's eyes that reminded Jimmie Cordie of a Chinese slave of Sahet Khan, the khan of the fierce, warlike Uryankhes Tartars. Jimmie knew that to the Chinese of the border cities, the Uryankhes were as demons.

"I will take them all," he said curtly, "and sell them to my blood brother, Sahet Khan of the Uryankhes Tartars. He knows how to treat degraded ones such as these." He spoke in Pushtu, loud enough for those in the line to hear. The old woman started wailing, and the relations in the rear joined in on general principles, not knowing what had been said.

That doom was entirely satisfactory to Changchau, the Manchus and the people of the city, and quite in keeping with the Big Sword reputation. "To be sold to the Uryankhes Tartars! Aie! What a fate! Better by far the torture at home than that which the Uryankhes would inflict. Aie! Aie!"

"Vot de hell und high vater is de idea in doin' dot?" demanded the Yid in English. "De Uryankhes vill skin dem alive und make it saddle—" Jimmie Cordie had turned and looked at the Yid. After a moment the Yid said loudly in Pushtu, "That is what we will do. We will sell them to the Uryankhes who will properly punish them."

"And the dogs of the Kirghiz who allowed the little mongrels of Nippon to join their caravan?" asked Changchau smoothly. "They are now being guarded by my swords."

"Put them outside your gates, unharmed," Jimmie ordered. "They know nothing of Nippon or of what the men of Nippon planned to do. You cannot afford a blood feud with the Kirghiz, Changchau. Because the men of Nippon came in with them, you have the right to put them out, fearing that there may be more of the men of Nippon among them. This the Big Swords will uphold against all in your behalf."

"You are right, war brother. There is no need of a blood—"

An officer came up and saluted. "The parties sent out to find the ones who escaped have come in, lord. There is no trace found."

The old woman and her relations were sent to the Uryankhes Tartars under escort of Big Swords. There is no question but what she and the relations passed some bad hours as far as worrying went before Sahet Khan laughed and ordered them all escorted to a Chinese city in the Kuen Lun range. This was after the Big Sword escort had started back.

Jimmie Cordie had sent a note written in English which he knew Sahet Khan spoke and read, asking that the Chinese be sent "in all honor" to the Chinese city and there turned loose after the war lord had been warned to treat them kindly.

And with that settled, Jimmie and the Yid headed back for their comrades, escorted by an honor guard of Chang-chau's finest men.

3

"OUT SWORDS!"

A CHINESE YOUTH stood in front of a table in the head-quarters tent of the main Big Sword encampment in the heart of the mountains.

At the table sat Chang-Lung Liang, leader of the Big Swords, head of the Manchu House of Chi.

The grim old face of the Manchu noble was as impassive as the face of a stone idol as he listened to the plea of the youth.

Behind Chang-Lung Liang stood several of the elder nobles of the House of Chi.

To the Japanese in Manchuria, or as they have renamed it, Manchukuo, the Big Swords were as a thorn in the side. The Japanese could handle any and all Chinese war lords who dared trying to block Japanese occupation of the country. But when it came to the Big Swords, the Japanese had to use all their strength if they wished to hold any territory within the sphere of Big Sword operations.

Jimmie Cordie had known and liked Chang-Lung Liang before the Manchu had become leader of the Big Swords, and when Chang sent for him to come, and help fight the Japanese, Jimmie came, bringing with him the other soldiers of fortune.

The Chinese youth, after he had been escorted into the tent, had bowed low and then tried to keep his knees from trembling. To him it was as if he had been put into a cage full of leopards. His grandparents had told him tales of the Manchus and now he, Kiong, stood close to them.

"You have my permission to speak, little one," Chang had said, not unkindly.

"I—I bear a message to you, mighty ruler of the world."

"Deliver the message and—do not tremble so, little one. You are safe with us. There are none here to hurt you. Be brave and speak the message firmly. You are under my protection."

That calmed the youth down a little and he began again. "I bear you a message, mighty lord, from the Lord Hukau, who holds the walled city of Fung-hwan. The words the Lord Hukau put in my mouth to utter are these: 'I fought for China, sparing nothing that I owned that would help me fight. I fought the men of Nippon at Sin-shan, at Tieling, at Pinvo, at Shol-choto and at Tsitsihar. I fought them always until my army became less than a regiment. Then I was first tricked and then deserted by my allies.

" 'I retreated to my city of Fung-hwan, followed by a pioneer regiment of Nippon. From a wounded officer of Nippon, whom I captured, I learned that the colonel of the regiment had been ordered to bring me to Nippon headquarters, dead or alive. I reached my city of Fung-hwan ahead of the Nippon regiment and am holding it.

" 'But I cannot withstand the attack much longer. There are many women and children and old men who must be fed and cared for. My ancestors for a thousand years were vassals of the House of Chi, and lived under the protection

of the House of Chi's banner. Now, I, Hukau, call pite-
ously on the House of Chi to protect me, its vassal. Come
quickly with the swords of Chi or we in Fung-hwan die at
the hands of the mongrels of Nippon.'"

"The city is surrounded, little one?" asked Chang.

"Yes, resplendent one at whose command sharp swords
are drawn."

"By how many of the little men of Nippon?"

"Why—I do not know exactly, ruler of the world. I heard
the Lord Hukau say to an officer that there must be at least
three thousand of the men of Nippon in the first charge
they made against the walls."

"What guns have they?"

"That I do not know, lord. I saw, from a slit in the wall,
some guns mounted on wheels that were moved from
place to place."

"How did you escape from the city?"

"I went through a hole in the wall when night came.
Then I crawled on my belly until I had passed through the
lines of the men of Nippon. Then I rose and ran, lord of
all swords."

"You have done well, little one. You may tell all men that
I, Chang-Lung Liang, head of the House of Chi, said so.
It is true that the ancestors of your lord were vassals of
the House of Chi, and so he is entitled to protection. The
House of Chi will give it to him. Captain Ting-chau, step
forward. You will take this youth to a place where he may
rest and receive care. You have my permission to depart."

After the Manchu officer had left the tent with the
Chinese youth, Chang turned in his chair and looked at the

remaining officers. Finally he said, "Step forward, Colonel Chuang Tzu—and you also, Major Lao Tzu."

Two of the Manchu officers stepped forward, two brothers. Colonel Chuang Tzu was the elder by six or seven years.

"I will honor you by sending you on a mission. This because of your excellent swordplay in the last engagement. You will take with you fifty swords of the House of Chi and locate Captain Cordie's flying column which is near the River Kokong where it dips towards the sea in the foothills. You will say to Captain Cordie that I ask that he go at once to the relief of the walled city of Fung-hwan which is being attacked by a Nippon pioneer regiment. He will destroy the little men of Nippon and bring all men, women and children in the city here. The War Lord Hukau and his fighting men may also come here if they desire to fight under my banner. If they do not, they may go elsewhere. Say to Captain Cordie that this is a matter that concerns the honor of the House of Chi. That is all. You have my permission to depart."

"WE HAVE THEM," a Black Mountain Uzbeg said gleefully. "We have them now. When they reach the cleared space below the spring we will put them to the sword."

Another Uzbeg beside him grunted as he looked through a cleverly arranged pile of dead branches at the fast approaching column of Manchus. "You are right, we have them. Let them get well into the clearing so that none may run away."

"You are young yet," the first speaker answered scornfully, "and do not know Manchus. Learn this: Manchus do not run away. They stand and fight to the death, always.

Draw back and pass the word that no attack is to be made before I rise. The dog brother that rises before I do will answer to me."

One hundred and fifty Uzbegs watched fifty-two Manchu swordsmen come up the mountainside towards a spring that one of the Manchus knew was there.

And Major Shima and Captain Noto, at the mouth of a little cave above the spring, also watched the Manchus. The two Japanese intelligence officers had escaped from the city and got to the hills by the grace of the gods of luck.

The Uzbegs did not know the Japs were there and the Japs did not know there was an Uzbeg within a hundred miles. So they both calmly watched the Manchus who did not know about either Jap or Uzbeg.

"If they come up to the spring," Captain Noto said, "we will be much better off in the cave. They will probably get a drink and then be on their way."

"I hope so," Major Shima answered. "It would be too bad if we were taken now after—in the cave, quick! We can see from there and still remain hidden."

Around the Manchus, completely circling them, there had risen Uzbegs, swords in hand.

The young Manchu colonel shouted, "Out swords! A wedge! I take the point!"

The Manchus did not have time to complete the wedge. The Uzbegs charged, yelling and shouting with glee. A good many of the shouts changed into death rattles as Manchu swords slashed home.

It was given the two Japanese intelligence officers, in the year of our Lord 1933, to see a sword fight in the hills between Manchus and Uzbegs. It was as if time had swung back a thousand years before guns and gunpowder were thought of.

The Uzbegs fought noisily, shouting threats to the Manchus and encouragement to each other. The Manchus fought silently, their lips tight, their eyes calm and cold, their faces impassive.

Man for man, the Manchus could have destroyed the Uzbegs who had unlimited strength but very little swordplay. But the Manchus were outnumbered three to one. In less than a half an hour there was a little circle of twenty Manchus, and around it there raged some fifty Uzbegs. All of the Manchus in the circle were wounded more or less, but their grim young faces were still impassive, and their eyes as cold as death itself and their lips tight.

"By the gods! What a fight!" Captain Noto said. "I have never seen such swordplay. It may be that the—no—the circle is broken!"

The Uzbegs had broken the circle and the fight became a mad swirl, then suddenly there was no more fighting.

Not an Uzbeg was on his feet, and of the Manchus, one man stood on his, swaying back and forth, bloody sword in hand.

He was Major Lao Tzu, honor graduate of the School of Swords.

HIS WOUNDS WERE not serious, consisting of several cuts where Uzbeg points had reached him. In the final flurry he had been struck on the head by a sword hilt in the hand of another Manchu who did not see him as the sword was swung up. The blow made him dizzy, but not so dizzy that he could not trick the Uzbeg in front of him into raising his sword for a parry. As it came up and out the Manchu blade cut through the Uzbeg heart.

"One left," Major Shima said, wetting his lips with his tongue. "One Manchu left and no—"

"See, he steadies himself and is—he is looking for something."

"He lifts a body in his arms and—he comes to the spring."

"We will ease down and hide behind those rocks. After we see what he intends to do we will take him. It may be that we can learn from him whether or not there are more Manchus between us and the river."

Major Lao Tzu carried his brother, who was mortally wounded, to the spring and there placed him gently on the ground.

As he started for the spring his brother raised himself on an elbow.

"No," he said distinctly, although there was blood trickling from his mouth. "No. Leave me and start at once for—"

"But Chuang, you are wounded, and will go on high if I do not bind your wounds. I cannot leave you to—"

"Attention—Major Lao Tzu. I speak—as Colonel Chuang Tzu and—and also as your elder brother. You will at once make your way to Captain—Cordie, and—the darkness comes. Hold me tight, Lao. I—I—no, I will not go—until—"

As he said "Captain Cordie" the Japanese officers looked at each other and smiled.

The young Manchu knelt and lifted his brother into his arms.

"That is better. I—command you to go—to go to

Captain Cordie and deliver to him the message—from—from—the Lord Chang. Say it that I may know—you have it correct. Quickly, Major Lao Tzu. I—sink—fast."

Major Lao Tzu repeated the message word for word, and the two Japanese intelligence officers heard it word for word.

"That—is—it. I go now to the chieftains, knowing that you—my brother—will— Out swords!"

The head of Colonel Chuang Tzu fell back as his gallant spirit left his body.

His brother looked down at the still face and sightless eyes for a moment, then eased the body to the ground and stood up. He looked down again for a moment, then saluted and said, "As you order, colonel."

After which he turned and went down the hill.

"Quiet," Major Shima said, as Captain Noto made a move as if to rise.

"But, I do not understand. Are you going to let him deliver that message to the Big Swords?"

"Certainly. He will deliver the message to Captain Cordie and at the same time we will deliver it to Colonel Nagayo who is at Haun with the Seventh Division. We will both get a step up, captain. It means a forced march for us but we win our way to Haun come what may."

4

BAD NEWS

THE FIGHTING YID, no matter where he was, could always produce cards and poker chips, and now, in the Big Sword camp at the river, he was banking a game of stud poker and at the moment, dealing.

"Come on, Red," the Boston Bean said, "it's your bet. Your eights are high. Why don't you do your sleeping in bed?"

"Don't rush me, Beany. I know 'tis my bet, but I misdoubt that Yid gibbon. He has an ace showin' and I think he has wan in the hole."

The Boston Bean looked at the Yid. "He better not have. The last five times he's dealt he's turned up an ace. I have a feeling that the sixth time will be fatal to Mister Cohen."

"Oi," mourned the Yid, "am I being accused of cheatingk at my time of life? Tell it to de Codfisher, Mistaire Dolan, dot I haven't a chick dot vould do such a trick."

"I will like hell, ye Hester Street scut. If ye turn up an ace this time it is me that will play the 'Wearin' Av the Green' on the coco av ye. Ye would cheat the grandmother av ye outta her specs if ye had to give them to her first."

A big, lean, broad shouldered man laughed. "They are

jealous of your superior skill, Yid." He was George Grigsby, ex-Foreign Legion and major of infantry, A.E.F.

"I'll bet two dollars on me eights, and wid it goes the warnin' that there will be wan less Yid clutterin' up the earth if ye have an ace in the hole, ye flat faced duck."

Jimmie Cordie came into the tent; with him was a slim, boyish looking man, John Cecil Carewe, ex-flight commander of a British air squadron.

"It looks as if the Yid were running true to form," Jimmie said with a grin. "Deal me in the next hand. I'll take those chips away from him so fast he will catch cold."

"How is your shoulder, Jimmie?" Grigsby asked.

"All right, thank you, George. It didn't go very deep. Anyway, it won't prevent me from cleaning Mr. Cohen."

As Jimmie sat down, a Manchu officer came in and saluted. Jimmie rose and returned the salute.

"Yes, Hsai?"

"Major Lao Tzu has just arrived, Captain Cordie. He is very weak from loss of blood and want of food, but insists that he deliver a message to you from the Lord Chang."

"I will go at once with you to Major Lao Tzu."

After Jimmie and the officer left the tent Red announced, "Something has come up."

"I think you are quite correct, Terence Aloysius, me good man," the Bean answered. "I also think our happy days of idle dalliance are over for the nonce."

"Whatever the hell that is. Why don't ye speak United States instead of that Bosting lingo, ye bean eater? And wance more, quit callin' me that 'me good man' thing or I'll take ye apart."

"Vait, let's play it de hand out, den I cash in," the Yid said.

They played the hand and the Yid won, not with a pair of aces, but with a pair of tens. "I don't need it aces to vin from a lot of suckaires like you," he stated as he raked in the chips. Which statement started an argument that lasted some time.

MAJOR LAO TZU delivered the message and then told what had happened to the Manchus of the flying column. After that he passed out of the picture for twenty-four hours.

"We will carry the wounded in litters," Jimmie Cordie said to the Manchu officers of the Big Swords. "Send men into the timber to cut sufficient poles and branches. We move out in two hours, gentlemen. Look out for Lao Tzu, will you, Carewe? Red, and you, Yid, get to the guns. Bean, take over the ammunition and supplies. Make it snappy, old kids. We're going to say good morning to Misto Jap at Fung-hwan in the cold gray dawn."

"Oi! How far is it, Jimmie?" asked the Yid.

"Fifty-odd miles, straight up and down, Mr. Cohen."

"Such a business. I am good for it, but I think dot maybeso Mrs. Dolan's little boy Red vill fall by de vayside, ain't it?"

"What! Me? Fall by the—"

"Tell him about it on the way to the guns," Jimmie interrupted. "And don't stop work while you are doing it, either. There are women and children behind the walls of Fung-hwan, don't forget that little thing."

" 'Tis right ye are, Jimmie darlin'. Come on, ye cross

between a gibbon and a black and white kitty, what are ye standin' there for?"

The Big Swords went through the hills. Not exactly straight up and down as Jimmie had said, but any mountain that could be climbed was climbed, and there was no hunting for easy paths. There were wounded and guns to be carried, plus ammunition and food. It was hard, gruelling work, and it wasn't long before Red and the Yid stopped telling each other things and buckled down to keeping the guns up where they ought to be.

Twice in the early part of the night there had come sudden whirlwind attacks on the column by hillmen who thought in the darkness they might have a chance. Each time the attack was met by the Big Swords and the attackers routed without hardly slowing up the march. The Big Swords in the column were picked men, and the soldiers of fortune, knowing that every minute counted, strutted their stuff.

The column went over the hills like a fire sweeps through dry timber, and anything in the way got out or perished.

ABOUT TWO O'CLOCK in the morning two Manchus of the far-flung advance guard brought in an elderly Chinese.

The story the Chinese told was this: He was fleeing before a Japanese army that was coming up from the south. At first, when he left his village he had tried to make An-si-fan to the west, but the Japs were there. He had doubled back and tried for Dadchin to the east, but the Japs were there also. To hear him tell it, the Japs were moving an army corps north.

Jimmie Cordie, knowing Chinese, discounted the number of Japanese troops, but knew that there must be a strong force heading, if not for Fung-hwan, at least in that direction. And if the Japs had no knowledge of Big Swords being in the immediate vicinity, their advance patrol would without question hear and very soon afterwards see the fight between the Big Swords and the Jap pioneer regiment at Fung-hwan—unless the Big Swords got there, mopped up on the pioneer regiment and then got the people of the city into the hills before even the patrols got near enough to hear and see. And Jimmie Cordie was under no delusions as to what it takes to mop up on any Jap regiment, pioneer or otherwise.

"When you fled your village where were the men of Nippon, venerable one?" he asked, one of the Manchus translating into Chinese.

"Within two miles, mighty captain."

"And your village is how far south of Fung-hwan?"

"Thirty miles, ruler of the world."

"Were the men of Nippon on the march?"

"When I fled, resplendent one. But when I came close to Dadchin, they had halted and made camp."

"Well, that will help some. I hope to high heaven they'll make a night of it. Ask him if he wants to stick with us or whether he'd rather be on his way. Tell him we are going to fight the men of Nippon."

The old Chinese promptly answered that he would rather be on his way as he was much too old to even look upon fighting, let alone try to do any of it.

After Jimmie had ordered that the Chinese be escorted to the north of the column, given food and turned loose, he said, "Well, for some unknown reason Misto Jap is taking a little stroll northward and by *muy malo* luck, Fung-hwan lies right smack in the path of the said stroll."

Jimmie had no way of knowing that instead of being by "very bad luck," the Japanese "stroll" was being made because of two Japanese intelligence officers and Colonel Nagayo of the intelligence.

This colonel had, in the past, twice tried for the soldiers of fortune who officered the Big Swords—and both times had been out-tricked and outfought by them. It had become a personal matter with him, and also with several other intelligence and military police officers, this trying to rub out Jimmie Cordie and his outfit. Not only for revenge, but because they thought that without the adventurers, Chang-Lung Liang and the Big Swords could be destroyed.

"We've got to get to Fung-hwan, chase the Japs away, get the populace out and into the hills before Misto Jap arrives in force or it will be just too bad—for us."

"That will all take time, Jimmie," Grigsby answered. "If they break camp at dawn, their advance guard will sight Fung-hwan by three or four o'clock. The Japs march fast and stay right with it. I don't know the country, but if it is like this, that's the outside time limit. And you know how much time it takes to get Chinese started out of a city where they have been born and raised. They want to take all the chickens and puppy dogs and kittens along."

"I know, George, yet the only thing we can do is to make the try."

"Dot ain't so good, either," the Yid said. "If ve make it de try de Japs is liable to catch us in de open between de city und de hills mit de vomen and children. Know vot dey vould do? Dey vould open fire on de whole cheese. I don't care for myself, und I hope dey do catch it Mistaire Dolan, de Irish gonif, in de open. But for de—"

"Oh, ye do? Ye hope they—"

"Put a jaw tackle on, Red. You're right, Yid, about that open fire thing. If we could get to a place where we could hole up, we might hold them back long enough for this bird to get his people to the hills, but if there was any way they could get around us they'd leave enough men to—"

"Too many 'ifs,' Jeems," the Boston Bean interrupted. "The old gentleman said that the Japs reached from An-si-fan to Dadchin. That means half a division, at least. The only thing we can do is—"

"To stop this damn wah-wah and get there," put in Red. "Is this an old ladies' debatin' society or is it a Big Sword column wid us leadin' it? To hell wid all 'ifs' or anything else. There's women and childers there. Let's go and get 'em out. To hell wid the little pink-toed banties. If they get in our way we'll slap 'em outta it."

Jimmie Cordie laughed. "Three cheers for the Dolans. Red has cleared the atmosphere. Get your running clothes on, gents. What you've had up to date is nothing to what you are going to get from this time on. The war cry will be 'to hell wid the little pink-toed banties.' *Allons, mes enfants! Boutez en avant!*"

WHEN THE "PUSH forward" started, the Yid eased alongside Red.

"Jimmie forgot to add it somethink to the three cheers for de Dolans. I vill add it for him, only instead of de vell known tiger—I add it de Bronx cheer—dere you are, Mistaire Dolan."

The noise the Yid made started Red on an oration concerning past and present Cohens, from the first one down to the Fighting Yid, that lasted at least a half hour.

It was five o'clock in the morning when the Boston Bean, looking cautiously around a rock up on the comb of a hill, said to Jimmie Cordie, "We made her, Jeems, me good man."

"We did," answered Jimmie, "and now that we have, we'd better get down there. It looks as if the Japs were going over the walls."

The walled city of Fung-hwan lay on a slope of ground that reached from the bank of a little river to a towering mountain. On three sides of the city the hills came to within a thousand yards. It had been built in the days when men fought only with swords, lances and bows and arrows, and in those days the walls had been, plus the fighting men inside, ample to protect it. But now, guns placed in the hills could knock the city into a cocked hat without any trouble.

The few guns the Jap pioneer regiment had with it had done a lot of damage, but were not heavy enough to make a breach in the walls. And the War Lord Hukau was still holding, in spite of repeated Japanese attacks. But his men were falling fast and Japs were beginning to come over the walls into the city. Up to the time the Boston Bean spoke, they had come over only to meet death. Hukau knew it was only a question of time before he would have no more men with which to stop the "little men of Nippon."

He did not know whether or not his call for help had got through to Chang-Lung Liang, and if it had, whether the Big Swords could reach him in time to save his city.

But he fought, he and his men, as a she-bear fights at the mouth of her cave, to protect her young.

"The next charge, war brother," he said to an officer beside him, "will be the last. See, they form to come on all sides."

"I see, Lord Hukau. Truly, as you say it will be the—"

Machine and rapid fire guns opened on the Japanese from the hills to the north. And a moment later, down from the hills swept a charge of Big Swords.

The Japanese were scattered out, divided into four units. The unit that was nearest turned and faced the fire from the hills and the Big Sword charge. There was no confusion or wavering. The Jap officers snarled a few commands and the unit tightened up to receive the charge.

It was a bad jam to be in and the Japs knew it from the officers down to the latest recruit. If they remained scattered out they had no chance to repel the charge. If they bunched, they offered that much better target for the machine and rapid fire guns. The guns were far away in the hills, and the charge was coming closer every second. The Jap officers knew that once the charge contacted, the guns would stop firing, so they met the charge, hoping that they could destroy it and then take the guns.

But the guns, operated by the Yid, the Bean, Red Dolan and Grigsby, veteran gunners all, and ranked among the first ten machine gunners in the Orient, with Jimmie Cordie and Carewe at the rapid fire guns, practically put the unit out of commission before the charge got halfway to it. And the Big Swords in the charge finished the job.

The two units to the east and west came around the walls on the double, and without a second's hesitation lowered their bayonets and charged the Big Swords. The Jap machine guns and rapid firers opened up. It became a regular Kilkenny cat fight inside of two minutes. Detachments of Big Swords were sent from the hills to take the Jap guns. They did, but few of the Big Swords came back to tell about it. The Big Sword guns had to quit firing because of the mixing up of Jap and Big Swords in a swirling dance of death.

THE FOURTH JAP unit, on the far side, started for the fight, on the run. But they had quite a ways to go before they cleared the wall. As they reached almost to the corner, a party of ten or twelve Jap cavalrymen rode out of the sparse timber along the river.

They beckoned frantically and two of them spurred their horses up to the unit commander. There was a few moments' talk, and then the unit, led by the two riders, ran for the timber. Not a retreat because, according to the Japanese, they never retreat. It was a "rearward" movement.

The cavalrymen had told of the Seventh Division advance guard being within four miles, and of the entire division being within ten. The Japs had not, as Jimmie Cordie had hoped they would, made a night of it. They had camped for a couple of hours, eaten and rested, and then resumed the march.

Jimmie Cordie lowered his glasses. "Did you see that, George?"

"See what, Jimmie?"

"Some Jap cavalry came out of the timber by the river and a couple of them rode up to the unit coming around the wall. Then they all high-balled it to the timber."

Grigsby smiled. "I reckon the well known wolf is at the

door. Three guesses, Jimmie, whether they camped last night or not."

"I don't need three. One will be plenty. If they don't outnumber us too badly we may be able to hold 'em off until Hukau can get to the hills with his people."

"I wouldn't bank too much on it, old kid. We can try it but—there go the Big Swords towards the city gates."

"That's her. Well, three Jap units have called it a day. Let's go, George. Time is of the well known essence, now."

The War Lord Hukau threw the gates of the city he had defended so well open to the Big Swords and they marched in. A few minutes later he stood with Jimmie Cordie and the other Big Sword officers, in the once beautiful flower garden in front of his palace.

"We have no time to talk about anything, Hukau," Jimmie Cordie said curtly in Pushtu. "There is a large force of Japanese moving up. Some of their advance cavalry is in the woods to the south at this minute. Get your civilian population together at once. In the hills we can hold the Japs back until you get to the Big Sword encampment."

"I have some fifteen hundred men, women and children here, Captain Cordie, and it will take some time to get them ready to march."

"It must be done with all possible speed, Hukau. They must leave everything here but the bare—"

An officer ran up. "The little men of Nippon come back, lord. From the river, the timber and the passes. See, they are already in the hills."

Jimmie Cordie looked up at the hills and saw Japanese guns being placed. "Get your people underground, Hukau.

It will be raining steel in a few minutes. How is your food and water supply?"

"I have plenty of both, Captain Cordie. The water comes from deep wells inside the walls, and before I came I ordered that all foodstuffs in the territory be brought into the city."

"All right. We have iron rations for two weeks so we will not have to draw on your supply. Get the food underground as far as possible. Japanese shells will be hunting for it very soon. How's your ammunition?"

"I have very little left, Captain Cordie."

"Hold your men in reserve for hand to hand fighting. We'll see what we can do to keep Misto Jap out."

5

BESIEGED

THE JAPANESE SEEMED in no hurry to attack. They placed their heavy guns in positions that commanded the city and their regiments kept well out of machine gun range. Jimmie Cordie and the Boston Bean, with two-pound rapid fire guns, shooting high explosive shells, tried for some of the guns, but the Japs put up heavy barricades of timber and went on about their business.

Finally Jimmie laughed. "No use wasting shells. I think we had better send Red up to slap 'em outta the way."

"Listen, Jimmie," Grigsby said, "we better try to get word to Chang that we are bottled up here in Fung-hwan by what looks like at least half of the Japanese Seventh Division. Once the Japs open fire they'll make this place look like the wreck of the Old Ninety-seven in an hour. And our ammunition won't last forever."

"To-night we'll try it. Two to Chang and two to the Uryankhes Tartars."

"Vot could be sveeter?" asked the Yid. "De Uryankhes smack dem in de hills und all de Big Swords on de right and left. Ve vould have it a grand stand seat und—"

The Jap guns opened fire so the soldiers of fortune never knew what the "und" was. And it wasn't much longer than

Grigsby had said before the city of Fung-hwan looked like the wreck of the Old Ninety-seven plus the wreck of several more trains. About noon the shelling stopped and the Japs sent a feeling-out charge. It was met by careful, accurate machine gun and rifle fire and wiped out before it got halfway to the wall. Then the big guns opened again, this time concentrating on the wall fronting the hills.

Like almost all of the old Chinese walled cities, Fung-hwan was honeycombed underground with passages and rooms. The Chinese did not dare to build outside the walls, and so, as their families and possessions grew, they got additional space by going below for it.

The Yid and the Bean, being more or less cursed with the uneasy foot, started out on an exploration trip.

There wasn't much to see, except Chinese crowded into rooms and wide passages and storerooms of food and whatnot until they came to what amounted to a big cave. At the entrance stood four or five Chinese soldiers, one of whom could speak some English.

"Vot is in dere?" the Yid demanded.

"The animals of the Lold Hukau, mighty genelal."

"Animals? Vot kind of animals? Has he got it a menagerie?"

"I do not know what a menagelie is, lesplendent one who leads the all powerful Big Swords."

"The resplendent one means animals who have been captured and tamed, little brother," explained the Bean.

"Yes, thele is a menagelie hele. Leopalds, wolves, beals and two tigels—also snakes flom India and other places."

"Ain't dot something, Beany? Und ve go in for nothing. Is it light enough to see dem?"

"We can make it light with tolches, leadel of millions."

"Do it den."

THAT JAPANESE GUNS were piling the city up over their heads into heaps of ruins, and that the city was entirely surrounded by men who would win promotion by producing the dead bodies of the soldiers of fortune— and intended to do it—made no difference to the Yid and the Bean. There was a menagerie to be seen, so they went in to see it.

Finally they came to a space, away from the other cages, where two big brown bears were chained by collar chains to stakes. When the Yid and the Bean, with the head keeper of the animals, who had come forward to greet them, halted, the bears got up on their hind feet and began a little shuffling dance.

"They ale tlained beals," the keeper said proudly. "Vely well tlained, but not vely fliendly, except to the Lold Hukau and me."

"My, dey is big suckaires, ain't dey?" the Yid said. "Go in und shake hands mit dem, Beany."

"What will you bet I dasn't?" answered the Bean, who loved animals, and as Grigsby said, "had a hand over them."

"Vot? I got it ten smackers dot says you von't, Mistaire Vinthrop. Von vill get you de ten if you shake it de hand of de big baby on de left."

"Get the ten out, my distinguished friend from Hester Street."

"Vait, Codfisher! I esk you!" The Yid said, for once in his life alarmed. "Don't did it. I vos only kiddingk."

"Caleful, lold," warned the keeper. "They ale not to be—"

The Boston Bean had taken two slow steps forward

and then stood absolutely still. He was well within reach of both bears. They stopped their dance and both snarled. The Bean stood as if carved out of stone. The Yid's .45 Colt appeared in his right hand as if put there by magic.

"No," the keeper said calmly, not raising his voice. "It is too late. You could not kill them both in time. Stand still. It may be that the blave one can—" again he stopped talking to watch.

Both bears went down on their fore paws, still snarling, and one of them, the biggest one, reached out and sniffed at the Bean's leg, then at his hand. The other backed away about a foot and then rose. The snarl of the one who sniffed changed into a querulous whine for a moment, then the Yid and the keeper saw something that really made the Yid's eyes pop with surprise. The bear rose up, put his paws on the Bean's shoulders and began lapping the Bean's face. The Bean slowly raised his right hand and cautiously scratched the ear of the nearest bear.

The other bear came up, his snarling stopped, took a couple of sniffs, rose on his hind paws and began the dance again.

"Vell—for de love of Mike!" the Yid said. "Dey think it dot de Beaneater is anodder bear."

"No," answered the keeper. "They smell a fliend, that is all, mighty one. A fliend who is unaflaid."

The Bean lifted the bear's paws and pushed the bear away, then gravely began the little shuffling dance himself. The bear watched him for a moment, then began to dance.

"Get it a collar und chain for de third bear. His name is Beany. In all my life I never seen it anythink like dot before."

The Bean danced over to the Yid and the keeper, then stood still.

"Produce the ten, Mister Cohen."

"I vill not. I bet it ten smackers dot you vould shake hands mit. All you did vos to dance. Give it me de von smacker."

"Well—you true son of all the Cohens. All right, I'll shake hands with both of them."

"Vait," the Yid said hastily. "Vait." He reached in a rear pocket and brought out a roll of bills. "I vos only standing it on de technicalities. Here is de ten mit my compliments."

"Yeah?" the Bean took the ten and put it in his pocket. "This will teach you not to dare old man Winthrop to shake hands with a bear."

AFTER THEY GOT back to where the rest of the adventurers were, the Yid told them about the Bean and the bears.

"Better not take any more chances, Codfish," Jimmie said. "We need your services at the moment. If those bears had got fussy about your coming to their dance uninvited, there would be one less machine gun go into action—not to mention the way we would feel about the Codfish Duke of Massachusetts being distributed around inside of two bears."

Suddenly he announced, "She's stopped. Get to your guns, gents. They'll try for us in earnest this time. No fooling around, Yid. That goes for you also, Codfish. Straight shooting and no fancy shots. Stay on your angles."

As they ran for their guns, the Yid asked peevishly, "Vy is it dot every time Jimmie says dot to us? Anyvon vould think dot ve do nothingk but take it pot shots."

"It may be, Mister Cohen, that he has caught us doing that little thing once in a while," answered the Bean gravely.

It is an easy thing to knock a walled city into ruins and to batter holes in a wall with big shells. But to take that city with infantry that must cross an open space to reach it is a horse of another color.

The guns put down a barrage but had to lift it sooner or later, and through it had come steel jacketed bullets from machine guns operated by men who were just as good scrappers as the Japs, if not better. And when the barrage lifted, Big Sword rifles opened up. Hukau's men crouched just back of the wall, waiting for any of the Japanese who got over.

But none did, that charge. When it was over, Jimmie Cordie looked at the ammunition left.

"Holy cats! Two or three more like that one and we'd do the rest of the fighting with swords and bayonets. And our little playmates don't seem to have any ideas about going home, either. How is your arm, Bean? I saw you favoring it a minute ago."

"Not so bad, Jeems. The bandage slipped and it started bleeding a little. I'm all right."

"Ye are not," Red stated firmly. "Come wid me, Beany darlin', and I'll fix it for ye. Does it hurt ye bad? Rest it on the shoulder av me."

"It is not that bad, thank you, Red, old-timer. Tighten this bandage and I'll be set."

"I'll twist the arm off ye if ye don't come wid me and let me fix it right, ye Codfish scut."

"That being the case, I guess I'll go with you, Mister Dolan."

As the Bean and Red walked away Jimmie said, "George, we'll try to run their lines as soon as it gets dark. It is the only chance we have. They are out to mop up on us this time, no foolin'."

"I say, you chaps, I'll make the try if you like," Carewe offered. "I'm not nearly as good with a machine gun as you jolly old blighters are and—"

"Oh, yes you are, Jonathan, just as good. And another thing, the Manchus are better than any of us, wiggling through lines. Thanks for the offer just the same. If Misto Jap isn't elbow to elbow, one of the four messengers may make the ripple. We'll instruct them all that Chang is to call upon Sahet Khan for help in my name or Sahet Khan is to call on Chang, and they are to gang up before attacking. If the Big Swords and the Uryankhes do get together I don't think that the whole Seventh Jap Division can stop them getting to us."

"Und if dey don't," the Yid said cheerfully, "ve fight it out mit de little pink toed banties right here."

"By request," Jimmie grinned.

"Right," Carewe said. "The giddy pink toed banties will know they've been in a fight after they have mopped up, what, what, what?"

"Doubly correct, Jonathan me lad," Jimmie answered. "And in the meantime we will—listen! Yeah, I thought so. *Adios, amigos, vaya con Dios.* Old man Cordie's son Jimmie is on his way to hole up, *pronto.*"

They all started for hole-ups, and it is a good thing for them that they did. A Japanese shell landed within ten feet of where they had been standing before any of them got a hundred feet away.

6

A WILY SCHEME

ABOUT MIDNIGHT FOUR Manchus slipped through holes in the walls. Two went south and two north—and an hour later their bodies lay in a row in front of Colonel Nagayo of the Japanese Intelligence and several of the Japanese line officers.

"So," Colonel Nagayo said, a smile on his lips. "Captain Cordie, the Yankee mongrel, sought to send word of his being caught in a trap to Chang-Lung Liang. That means that at last he has lost his cocksureness."

"The two that were slain at the river were heading away from the Big Sword encampment, colonel," a major volunteered. "More towards the territory of the Uryankhes Tartars."

"What difference does it make?" snarled Colonel Nagayo. "Now the bodies of the Manchus, who think themselves superior to all other races, lie here at our feet. We have the Yankee curs and the Englishman, Carewe, at last in a trap where their tricks will not avail."

A young Japanese captain stepped forward and saluted smartly.

Colonel Nagayo barely returned the salute as he rasped, "What is it, Captain Nugata?"

"This, colonel. When Major Kiushu spoke of the Uryankhes Tartars, it reminded me of something."

"And you, a captain of infantry, take up my time to tell me what it reminded you of, do you?" sneered Colonel Nagayo.

The young officer's face flushed but he answered, "I remembered that I had heard that Captain Cordie of the Big Swords had undergone the blood brotherhood rites with Sahet Khan of the Uryankhes Tartars."

"I know that, Captain Nugata—as does every other well informed officer. What of it?"

"May I ask you a few questions, colonel? They will aid me in making my plan clear."

"I have no time to waste answering—yes, you may ask me a few questions, Captain Nugata. See to it that they are pertinent ones."

"Captain Cordie believes that the Uryankhes Tartars would come to his rescue if they knew his need?"

"He knows that the Uryankhes Tartars would, Captain Nugata."

"Then, if to-night he heard the Tartar yells in the hills and machine gun and rifle fire answering, what would he think?"

Colonel Nagayo stared at the young captain for a moment, then his lips parted in a smile. His voice was much more pleasant as he answered, "He would think that his friends the Uryankhes were coming to the rescue, Captain Nugata."

"We have three cavalry regiments, colonel. Could they not, for the moment, be Uryankhes Tartars? If finally they broke through our lines and rode to the city walls, what would Captain Cordie do?"

"He would open the gates for them. But the first weak point in your plan, Captain Nugata, is that the Uryankhes Tartars would come to his rescue with many more riders than three thousand odd."

"Would he not think that his messengers had met, say a flying column of Uryankhes Tartars on their way home or, it may be, on their way to scout out what the presence of so many Nippon troops this far north means? Knowing the Uryankhes Tartars as he must know them, would he not think that they would at once ride to the rescue, regardless of odds against them?"

Colonel Nagayo studied for a minute, then answered, "Yes, he would think that, Captain Nugata."

"And so, thinking that, he would open the gates for all of them that got through our lines, knowing that if he did not, we would destroy them."

"Yes, he would open the gates for them. You have strengthened the first weak point, Captain Nugata. Let me see if you can also strengthen the second weak point. Transform our cavalry into Uryankhes Tartars. Remembering that the Uryankhes Tartars are big, hairy men."

"Why, that is not—is not up to me, colonel. There are officers present who have had experience in camouflage that—"

The colonel of one of the cavalry regiments stepped forward, his eyes shining. Here was a chance to win glory and promotion. "I can make my regiment look like the Uryankhes Tartars," he stated. "Stirrups can be shortened, many rope bridles can be substituted, sheepskin coats can be worn, hay and straw can be used to bind the feet and legs and—and hair from the tails and manes of our horses will make us as hairy as the Tartars. In the darkness who can detect us? I have men, and so have Colonels Figami and Jamada, who can speak—and yell—the Tartar language. Once inside the gates we, the cavalry will take the city and the mongrel adventurers."

Colonel Nagayo was not quite as sure as the cavalry colonel about the last statement. He had had two or three bitter experiences with the Big Swords, and he knew how they could and would fight.

"If you can hold the gates open and keep the Big Swords occupied until the infantry gets there, colonel, you will have done your part. Let us plan, gentlemen. Whatever is done must be done before the break of dawn. Captain Nugata, I will request that you be detailed to me, as reward for your suggestion and also request that you be advanced to the rank of major. Now, the regiments must be scattered through the passes and the timber. After the units break through our lines, they come together and ride for the gates, yelling and shouting. There must be many riderless horses with them and...."

THE NIGHT WAS a dark one, most of the time. The moon was out, but heavy clouds were passing between it and the earth. Every once in a while, as one cloud cleared the moon and before another came, the moonlight made things fairly light.

Jimmie Cordie, Hukau, Red Dolan, Carewe and several Manchu officers were on the wall over the gates which were made of heavy timber reinforced with thick copper bands. Leading into the city from the gates there was a fairly wide street that only went a hundred feet or so, dead-ending at a stone wall in which there were two smaller gates. Shells might batter down the big gate, but there were other gates and walls to demolish and take before entering the city proper.

Machine gunfire and a moment afterwards rifle fire was heard to the north.

"Some one has stirred our little playmates up," Jimmie said with a grin. "Maybeso a black and white kitty has—hear that? Uryankhes Tartars! Listen! The Manchus must have met them and—"

"They're comin' in all the passes!" Red interrupted. "Will ye listen to them tellin' the little pink toed banties all about it!"

Yells and shouts could be heard plainly, getting more and more distinct every moment. Machine guns opened fire all along the Japanese northern lines.

"Wait a minute, Red," Jimmie Cordie interrupted, "I want to listen to—"

The moon shone brightly for a minute, long enough for the men on the wall to see, coming out of one of the lower passes, a group of some two hundred riders who were standing in their stirrups, yelling and waving swords about their heads. With the group were thirty or forty riderless horses.

There is no question but what, in the distance and moonlight, the Japanese cavalry looked like Tartars. The cavalry colonel had certainly spared no pains in the camouflage.

"Jimmie! Here they come! Let's go out and meet them."

"What did you say, Red?" Jimmie answered, absently. "I was—"

Clouds came over the moon again and Jimmie stopped talking for a moment, listening to the yells that now came from several of the passes that led to the mouth of the one main pass to the hills.

"Jimmie! Order the gates open. What the hell is the matter wid ye?"

Jimmie Cordie laughed. "I've been taking a little cat nap, Red. Open the gates, Hukau, and light—" The moon came out again and Jimmie looked up at it. "Never mind about bonfires on the wall. Lady moon is going to furnish us light for a little while."

The Japanese had set the stage well, and each unit played its part as if trained for days instead of minutes. As the synthetic Uryankhes Tartars came out in the open they were followed by Japanese infantry who fired on them. Men threw themselves from the saddles as if wounded or dead. Machine and rapid fire guns kept up an incessant fire and back in the hills was more yelling.

NOW THE JAP riders, two thousand odd, bunched as they cleared the hills and in a disorderly column rode for the gates, shouting and yelling.

"See, the gates are open to us," a Jap officer said to the officer who rode on his right. "We have tricked them."

"Once in, we will do more than trick them—"

He did not live to finish his sentence. A blasting fire from machine guns, rapid fire guns and rifles opened on the Japanese from the walls of the city.

It turned the fast riding, shouting column into a bloody shambles of dead and dying men and horses. And the city gates closed.

There was silence in the hills for a moment, and then

every Japanese gun opened up. In half an hour the shelling stopped and regiment after regiment charged on all sides.

It was dawn before the Japanese realized that, as yet, they could not put a man over the walls and the attack ceased.

Red Dolan came up to Jimmie Cordie. "Jimmie, how did ye know they wasn't the wild men?"

"Well, first, Mister Dolan, you will admit that the Uryankhes Tartars are big, deep chested men?"

"I will. What has that got to do wid it, ye shrimp av the world?"

"I'll do the questioning, Terence Aloysius. You do the answering. Second, have you ever heard a Uryankhes Tartar shout, 'Ho, brothers! Cut! Slash! Slay!'?"

"I dunno whether I have or not. I have heard many wild men yell, if that's what ye mean."

"Well, the Uryankhes Tartars and the Altai and the rest of the hillmen are big, and as I said, deep chested men. When they shout or yell it sounds like the bass of a pipe organ all het up. There are no reedy tenors among the Tartars.

"At first the yells sounded all right to me, because I was thinking of something else. Then I caught a note or two that did not sound sweet at all to me. They were more like the squeak of a dying titmouse than they were like a Uryankhes Tartar roar. Then, when they began pouring out of all the small passes and the timber and whatnot, that didn't look at all good to me, either."

"Why didn't it?"

"Well, the small passes here lead to the mouth of the main pass no matter what side they are on. The Uryankhes Tartars would come down the main pass to get at the

Japs and—listen, Red, the Uryankhes only charge one way, and that is straight ahead. They don't scatter out and try for weak points in a line. They would come down the main pass hell for leather with the one idea of riding over whatever was between them and their objective, and they'd stick together also. They wouldn't try to get through other passes or do anything else trained troops would do. They'd only think of where they wanted to go and head for it. Are you keeping up with me, Mister Dolan?"

"I am. Go on."

JIMMIE SAID, "FINE. Now I will tell you what made me doubly suspicious. There was too much machine gun and rifle fire in the hills, and the Japs that showed and fired on the riders did not empty enough saddles. Misto Jap doesn't miss like that, Red. Are you fully informed now why I opened fire?"

"I am. Lucky for us that ye knew the difference between the het up bass of an organ and the squeak av a titmouse, ye small sized, half pint av nothin'."

Jimmie Cordie laughed, "Go on away from me, you red-headed ape. I've got to get busy."

Red grinned and left to see if he could locate the Boston Bean and the Yid.

Jimmie Cordie walked over to where Grigsby was super-intending some repairs on the east wall.

"I didn't think Misto Jap had it in him," he said as he sat down. "From now on we'll have to watch our step, George."

Grigsby smiled. "He had me fooled, Jimmie. I would have received the Uryankhes Tartars with open arms— and got a bayonet between them for my hospitality. It was clever, at that."

"Yeah, darn good and clever. But the gent that planned it forgot or didn't know a couple of small things. Like planning the perfect crime, I guess. There is always something that slips. I wish to high heaven we could think of something that would decoy our gentle little boy friends down on the next street for a day or so."

"So do I. We are losing men fast, Jimmie."

At eight o'clock in the morning the Japanese guns opened fire for a few minutes. Then they suddenly were still and a small party came out of the nearest timber, carrying the bodies of four men. They advanced on the double for a hundred yards or so, laid the bodies down in a row, and ran back to the shelter of the timber.

Jimmie Cordie, who had been watching through his glasses, lowered them. "The Nine Red Gods decided against us," he announced. The bodies were the bodies of the four Manchus who had tried to run the Jap lines.

As he said it, the guns opened again, this time all of them at once.

The attack that came, after hours of bombardment, was repulsed, but not until quite a few Japs had got into the city through the holes in the walls. They were met and destroyed by Manchu swords, led by Tseng Wang.

"I guess dey have quit foolingk around mit us," the Yid said as he cleaned his machine gun. "Are you going to send it out some more messengers, Jimmie? Maybeso I could make it to de river und svim under water past de Japs. Vonce I got in de hills I could make it to de Uryankhes, I bet you."

"I'm afraid you couldn't swim under water long enough to get by them, Yid. No, if Manchus can't win through, any one of us wouldn't stand a chance. Only thing we can do is to ask for volunteers among them to try it again to-night."

"Oi, Jimmie! I have thought it of something."

"Well, for Pete's sake, open up."

"Vait till I go und talk mit de Codfisher. Den I tell you. Maybeso it vould vork."

7

THE CRAZY AFGHAN

THE YID FOUND the Boston Bean, who had disappeared right after the Jap attack had been stopped, down where the Bean spent most of his odd moments, with the two big bears. By now they had accepted the Bean as a royal play-fellow. The Bean could put them through a series of tricks that made the head trainer shake his head in astonishment.

"Come avay from dem," the Yid commanded. "I vant to talk mit you for a minute."

"Some other time, Mister Cohen, if you please. I am very busy and—"

"I don't please. Dis is strictly business, Codfisher, und Jimmie is vaiting."

"That's different. Good-by Grizzly and Polar."

"Vot de hell do you call it dem dat for?" demanded the Yid as he and the Bean hunted for a place to sit down.

"Because they are not that kind of bears," explained the Bean gravely.

"You know vat I think? I think dot you are goofy—und at dot, it vill help if you are."

"Help what?"

"Vot you are going to did, Beany."

"Oh, yeah? And what am I going to do, Mister Cohen?"

"Listen now und don't interrupt poppa until he is all through. You remember de time dot ve vos in Sanshu mit de var lord Hing-San ven de birthday celebrations of his son vos being held?"

"Very well, indeed, Mister Cohen. I remember also that you got hold of some brandy and got pie-eyed drunk. Double shame on you for doing 'er, also."

"I did not," protested the Yid. "I vos sick, dot's all. But dot is neither here nor dere. You remember de emir of de vorld dot came mit de trained bears?"

"I remember the bears. Do you mean the goofy Afghan that owned them?"

"Yes, de emir of de vorld. Anyway dot is vot he said he vos. Remember how de Chinks made it vay for him because he vos a goofy?"

"Blame few people will hurt a crazy man, Yid. A good many races think he is under the protection of the gods who have taken some of his brain for their own use."

"Vell," said the Yid slowly. "Maybeso de Japs vouldn't hurt—or stop—a goofy, either."

"Maybe they wouldn't. But what has that to do with what you said was—" The Bean stopped talking for a moment, then grinned and said, "Maybeso can do, Yid. Let's go talk to Jeems."

Jimmie, Red Dolan, Carewe and Grigsby listened to the Yid and the Bean and finally Jimmie shook his head. "I don't think you'd have the chance of a lame dog in a running match, Codfish. The Japs would knock you and the bears off the Christmas tree first and then wonder if you possibly might have been crazy afterwards.

"I don't doubt for a moment but what you can play the

part of a goofy Afghan, but—can you dress yourself up to look like one?"

"Why can't he?" demanded Red. "Right now he is a goofy Beaneater from Bosting, and 'tis not much difference between a—"

"Listen, you red-headed ape, is this the time to get funny? The Bean is offering to bet his life that he can get through the Japs as a crazy Afghan with two bears. It's a hundred to one shot that he can't do any such thing. Do me a favor and go somewhere and think that over if you can't keep that mouth of yours shut."

" 'Tis right ye are, Jimmie darlin'. Don't try it, Beany. Ye know how much we all think av—I'm shut, Jimmie."

"I don't think the odds are that bad, Jeems," the Boston Bean said. "If the Japs are like other people, the odds are in my favor that they will pass me along with a laugh."

"That's just it. I don't think they are—in lots of ways. Maybeso civilians, yes. But not the military, old kid. They are all soldier and nothing else. And personally I can't see them passing any one or anything along through battle lines."

"But you don't know that they will not pass a crazy Afghan with a couple of trained bears through, do you?"

"No. I don't know that, Codfish."

"Well, then, why not try it?"

"Because in making the try—which I think is a useless one—we would probably lose the famous Codfish Duke of Massachusetts."

"Which does not amount to a tinker's dam against the fact that if it works the lives of women and children may be saved."

FOR A LONG minute there was silence after the Bean said that. The faces of the soldiers of fortune became grim and impersonal as did their eyes.

Jimmie Cordie, looking straight at the Bean, began to whistle softly, "There is a fountain filled with blood drawn from Emanuel's veins. And sinners—" When he got that far he stopped whistling and said, "That's right, John. Your life or any of our lives do not amount to a tinker's dam, if women and children are to be saved. I vote that you try it."

"So do I," Grigsby said quietly.

"And I," Carewe said.

" 'Tis a hard thing to say," Red began, "knowin' that ye go to the death av ye, Beany darlin'. Me vote is like the rest. Go and try it, and may all the good saints take care of ye."

As the Yid and the Bean went underground, the Yid said cheerfully, "Vell, ve put it over, didn't ve, Codfisher?"

"We did. Do you remember how the emir of the world looked? I mean in general?"

"I do, mit great clearness. He vos tall und skinny, like you, mit long straggly black hair falling all over his face und eyes und a couple of feathers sticking in it, held dere by a ivory comb. His face und hands vos dirty und his clothes vos a collection of rags dot an old clothes man vould turn de nose up at. Und on his feet vos a pair of old sandals held dere by string, und on his—"

"That's plenty to start off with. Let's see how close we can come up to it, including the sandals before we go any further. We can get the black hair from a Chinese woman.

"The Japs used horsehair, but we will go them one better."

IT WAS QUITE a little later when the Yid announced to

Jimmie Cordie and the rest, "Ve are ready for de inspection. Come mit to de menagerie."

They went "mit" to the menagerie, and when they arrived in front of the bears, Red said, "Holy Saints! If that is Beany, he is more of a goofy Afghan than the real wan is."

The Boston Bean's architectural lines had helped a lot in making him look like a goofy Afghan or a goofy hillman of any breed. He and the Yid had commandeered any and all things they thought were needed both for the main part of the costume and for artistic touches.

All in all, the Codfish Duke from the top of his head to his toes looked the part.

Right after Red spoke, the Bean let out a howl that was a cross between the scream of a hungry mountain lion and the wail of a northern wolf telling the moon of his sorrows. Then he began yelling in Pushtu, "Way! Way for the emir of the world and his children! Kneel in front of me, slaves! Kneel or my children shall devour you! I am the emir of the world, and all men are my slaves! Way! Way for the emir and his children! We go to the birthday festival of the son of the Khan of the Altai Tartars!"

And while he was yelling it, he and the bears were doing the little shuffling dance.

As the Bean and the bears, the Bean holding them by the collar chains, were ready to go through a hole in the wall that faced the river, Jimmie Cordie said, "Don't start, Codfish, until you hear us cut loose. And then wait a minute or two. The river bank looked clear dead ahead this afternoon, and it may be clear yet. If you get that far you've jumped the first hurdle. Maybeso the Japs along the river will scatter out a little to take a looksee at what is going on in front. That's all, Bean. Good huntin', old kid."

"I'll make 'er, Jeems, me good man. And if I don't, I'll wait with Put for the rest of the gang to show up. Never mind any farewell speeches. Get going on that sortie thing. This darkness may not hold. I'll be seeing you."

"Not wan damn step will I go," Red declared, "until I have said this. Good luck, and may all the saints take care av ye, Beany darlin'. 'Tis a stout feller ye are, when all is said and done."

"Und dot goes for me," the Yid added.

"And for me"—"And for me," Carewe and Grigsby said.

"And also for me," Jimmie Cordie stated. "Let's go!"

THE GATES OF the city suddenly were flung open and a column of the Big Swords came out. As the column cleared the gates, machine guns opened from the walls, concentrating on a pass from which Japanese infantry had issued during the day. The Japanese machine guns instantly answered and flares were sent up.

"The dogs try to cut their way to the hills," a young Japanese officer said to another.

"We will stop them before they have come a hundred yards. Truly they have gone mad when they think they can reach our lines."

"The machine gunfire from the walls shows that the ones Colonel Nagayo wants so badly are not with—here comes the Taiku regiment! To your post, Lieutenant Akita."

The Big Swords column advanced rapidly almost up to the Japanese flares, then as the Taiku regiment deployed so that the column might have room to get well inside the lines before the Japs closed the gap, they swerved to the left, turned, and ran back to the gates and into the city.

"What kind of maneuver was that?" asked the Japanese officer, puzzled. "They lost many men by our machine gunfire, and yet—they did not even try to close with us. I thought that the Big Swords were mostly Manchus who always charged home."

"The Manchus do charge home—unless ordered otherwise. The Yankee mongrels who are trapped in the city are trying some kind of a trick. It will fail, as ours failed, whatever it is. This time we have them in a place where tricks will not work," an officer answered.

The Japanese officer was wrong; the trick had worked. The Japanese unit on guard at the river bank directly in front of the south wall had run along the bank until they could see the flares; and there they had stood for a few minutes. And while they were doing it, the Bean and the bears reached the bank of the river. There he waded in up to his neck, and after a little coaxing, got both bears in the water for a moment or so, then came out and started up the river bank.

The bears, delighted at being in the open once more, tugged at the chains and the emir of the world had all he could do to hold them.

He had not gone two hundred yards before there came a snarled command from the darkness ahead. His Japanese was absolutely nil, but any man who has served in any army knows a command to halt when he hears it, no matter what language it is delivered in.

The Bean halted and let out a yell that Jimmie Cordie and the others heard in the city.

Then he began his "Way! Way for the emir of the world."
For a moment or more there was silence in the darkness
ahead and then a flare turned the darkness into the light
of day.

The Bean danced up to the flare with the bears, still
yowling about who he was and what would happen if way
were not made for him. And before he got very far he and
the bears were inside a ring composed of Japanese bayonets. The Bean, as he drew breath, thought, "By golly, they
didn't shoot. I've got 'em!"

A non-commissioned officer, his revolver full on the
Bean, demanded in Pushtu: "Who are you, and how did
you get to the river bank?"

The bears did not like the ring of sharp points that
surrounded them, and also did not like the smell of the
men back of the points. They both looked at the Bean and
then began snarling.

"You see?" he yelled. "You see, slaves? My children are
getting angry. Beware! Beware! Soon I will order them to
eat you up. I am the emir of the world and at my command
the stars and the moon will fall to crush you! Down on
your knees, slaves, and worship me and my children who
are kings of all kings! Bring food at once and drink that
we may refresh ourselves."

He heard several of the Japs say one word, which he
hoped was "crazy" in Japanese.

The non-commissioned officer gave a curt order and
the circle widened out as he stepped forward. Not so far
forward as to be within reach of the bears.

"Where do you come from, brainless one?"

"From everywhere!" yelled the Bean. "From the sun!

From the moon! From the lowest depths of hell—where I will send you very soon! From the river where I swam for miles with my children."

"You swam up the river, you and your children? I see you are wet. It may be that is the way you came through our lines. And where are you going—emir of the world?"

"I go to the Altai Tartars who are slaves of mine, as you are! Down on your knees and worship me! I am—"

ONE OF THE bears made a lunge at the Jap who stepped quickly back, raising his revolver, which he had lowered. The Bean had hard work for a second or so, calming down the bear. He did it, though, and then began to dance. After a little hesitation the bears joined in. The Japanese soldiers crowded closer.

An officer pushed his way through them, looked at the Bean and the bears, then demanded, "What is the meaning of this, Sergeant Shin-ju?"

"If the captain please, this crazy Afghan and the bears suddenly appeared on the river bank. I have been trying to find out where he came from. He tells of swimming up the river and of his being on his way to the Altai Tartars. I did not order that he be slain because, as the captain sees, he is crazy."

"The noise he is making will wake Colonel Kona, and then he will receive short shrift, crazy or not. Calm him down and take him to the guardhouse for the rest of the night. In the morning the colonel will decide what to do with him."

The Bean was gravely dancing with the bears, knowing that his fate was being discussed. He thought that he had better do no more yelling at the moment.

The non-commissioned officer saluted, the captain returned the salute and walked away. As the non-com turned to the Bean, the emir of the world said to himself, "Here she comes."

"Come with me. You and your children shall receive shelter and food."

"Three cheers for that," the Bean said to himself, then aloud answered, "I will honor you, slave. Lead the way!"

Once in the guardhouse, which was a big one-room log cabin the Bean felt that the three cheers had been called for a little prematurely. And he felt it more strongly after food and water had been brought and he heard the heavy door lock after the two Jap soldiers who had served it.

He had got this far without being killed but it wasn't so very far, at that.

The bears seemed quite content, both of them curling up and going to sleep. The emir of the world stayed awake, putting in the time regretting that in his younger days he had not taken up the study of the Japanese language. If he had he might have known what the Jap captain said to the non-com.

ABOUT FOUR O'CLOCK in the morning the door opened and several Japanese officers came in. None of them had any suspicion that the crazy Afghan was a synthetic one. They wanted to see him and the bears for the same reason the soldiers did—anything to break the monotony of guard duty.

The Bean rose and let out a yowl that surpassed all his previous ones. He knew that this was the crucial moment and if he did not make it stick now he would never get another chance.

"You dare to come unsummoned into my presence, slaves! I will order the moon and the stars to fall upon—" that was the last of the Bean's impersonation. Both bears woke up and rose on their hind legs snarling. The Bean reached down to get hold of the chains and as he did, the biggest bear made a pass at him, whether in play or in earnest he did not know.

The claws raked the top of the Bean's head and carried away with them the dirty fillet of cloth that helped hold the black hair in place. The hair had been glued to the Bean's scalp by the Yid and then the narrow strip of cloth had been added in a way that did not prevent the hair from falling around the Bean's face. And with the cloth there went most of the hair.

The Jap officers stepped back and drew their revolvers. One of them shouted, "The Boston Bean!" and fired point blank at the Codfish Duke of Massachusetts. By mischance he had been one of the Jap officers who had attempted to take the soldiers of fortune once before and had been wounded by the Bean at close quarters. He had never forgotten the Bean's face, both front and profile and now he recognized him.

One of the bears had started after the Japs and the bullet meant for the Bean hit the bear in a fleshy part of the shoulder. The bear roared his protest and charged with outstretched paws.

The other, without a second's hesitation, also roared a challenge and charged. The Jap officer flung himself backwards and in doing so overturned the oil lamp that set on a wall shelf.

The charge of two big bears is not to be faced in any

room by men armed with revolvers and the Japs knew it. They backed to the door, emptying their guns as they did so. The bullets hit but did not stop the bears any more than a stone thrown by a child would. The bullets did not have the power to penetrate to a vital spot. They only made the bears more infuriated. Two of the officers failed to get out and both died there, their bodies torn open by steel-like claws.

The bears, roaring defiance, charged out after the officers and the guardhouse began to blaze. Soldiers came running up with bayoneted rifles and there in the darkness, until flares were lighted, there began a bear fight that the Japs talked about for quite a while afterwards.

The bears were big and their vital parts well cushioned with fat and muscle and, like all bears, scrappers when they once got started. They took bayonets and rifle and revolver bullets for a long time before they went down to stay down and Jap after Jap who got too close went down before the bears did. It was a messy, noisy fight, the Japs shrilling encouragement to each other above the roars of the bears and the gunfire.

Jimmie Cordie, standing near a pile of rock that had once been a temple near the south wall, listened intently for a moment, then said to Grigsby who was there with him, "I guess we celebrated the Bean getting through a little too soon, George. He was either holed up or the Japs were looking him over. The bears are trying to lick the Jap army by the sounds. I guess it means that the odds were too great for the Codfish Duke."

"I'm afraid it does, Jimmie. He was a brave— They attack again!"

8

HAND TO HAND

THE JAPANESE HAD decided that the breaches blown in the walls were large enough. Now they were going to take the city and wipe out the Big Swords and the Chinese who defended it. And this time they got to the walls and through the holes in spite of the withering fire that spat defiance at them.

Jimmie Cordie ordered flares and big bonfires lighted along the walls and on top of piles of ruins. He knew that the Jap guns in the hills could not open fire for fear of hitting their own men once the Japs had got to the walls and he wanted light enough to, as he told Tseng Wang, "give the swords of the House of Chi a chance to see the little men of Nippon die by Manchu swordplay."

To the Japanese on the hills it looked to be a city on fire surrounded far out by a ring of darkness from which emerged a steady stream of bayonets.

There were two large breaches in the wall, both some hundred feet wide, and many smaller ones. Jimmie Cordie placed machine guns and what rapid fire guns he had at both of the lower breaches and at the smaller, Hukau's riflemen. The Big Swords were split up into units and placed all along the walls.

The Yid and Red were at one of the breaches with the machine guns, Grigsby and Carewe at the other. Several of the Manchus had been taught how to operate rapid fire guns and machine guns and now, as Jimmie Cordie put all reserve guns in commission, had a chance to show how much they had learned from the experts who had been their teachers.

The Japs came through and over the walls like men hurrying to what they knew would be a gay, pleasant party.

But in doing it they took losses that would have staggered any commander who did not firmly believe that soldiers were made to be killed in battle.

Red and the Yid had been told about what Jimmie Cordie and Grigsby had heard, Red and the Yid being underground asleep at the time of the bear fight. Carewe had heard most of it from his post of duty.

The first Japs through the large breaches did not hesitate a second. They charged the machine guns. But their charge was met by Manchu swordsmen before they reached the guns. At the smaller holes the Japs shot and bayoneted their way through Hukau's men, only to meet the Big Swords.

Those of the Japs who came over the walls, as they jumped to the ground, also faced the Big Swords.

Grigsby and Carewe fought their guns, as did the Manchus, calmly and coldly, as if they were on the target range. Jimmie Cordie went from place to place, a smile and a jest on his lips and in his eyes—and a Colt .45 in his right hand. In the Orient, whenever soldiers of fortune gathered for a little chin-chin and the talk veered around to good shooting, some one, sooner or later would ask, "Did you ever see Jimmie Cordie strut his stuff with a .45 when he got down to business? That bird can shoot the eye outta a needle at two hundred yards." Which was a slight exaggeration but there was no question about Jimmie Cordie being a first class shot.

RED AND THE Yid also fought their guns, but neither calmly nor coldly. Red was almost berserk and as he fired was yelling, "So ye got Beany, did ye? Ye ganged up on him and pulled him down. I'll make ye wish a wolf had stolen ye from the cradle!"

The Yid was talking but not good naturedly as he generally talked while fighting. This time he was, as he said later, "damn good und mad mit dem." His talk was a running comment on what he thought of all Japanese and how much he would love to send them all to the southwest corner of the hot place and then order a northeast gale to blow.

Finally Red jammed his gun, whether purposely or not there was no way of telling. "Now I'll get me a sword," he yelled, gone all the way berserk, as he stood up. " 'Tis what I wanted all the time."

He did not have any trouble in finding a sword. There were more than a few Manchu swords on the ground or still held in the lifeless hands of their owners. Once Red had one in his hand he let out a wild Irish yell and joined the nearest Manchu unit.

The Yid stayed with his machine gun for a minute or so and then as an infantry company came through the breach and started up the pile of rocks, the Yid, without waiting to see if Manchu swords came to block the Japs off, slid down the other side of the pile and hunted for a sword himself. He found one and joined Red Dolan.

Jimmie Cordie, as the machine guns stopped, ran up to see what had happened. He got there just in time to see the swords close with the Jap company, the Yid and Red right in front.

More Japanese were coming through, company after company now, and Jimmie saw that there was no hope to get to either machine gun and try to stop them. He ran back to where a Big Sword reserve was being held on that side and brought them up along the wall to the breach. Then, leading them, he started for the other end of the breach, right through a Jap company.

The Big Swords won through and then turned and faced the coming Jap.

The night was sultry and the air pressed down like a wet blanket. As the Japs charged the sword line, there came first lightning and right after it seemed as if the heavens had opened. A cloudburst in the Thian Shan puts everything within range out of commission and a good deal of everything except the hills under water. It put out all flares and bonfires and stopped all fighting as promptly as turning off a radio dial stops a program. Any living thing caught in it has all it can do to keep on breathing.

The Japs between the walls and the hills dropped and hugged the ground until water coming down the hills and the passes forced them to get up and try for higher ground. Some made the foothills, but many did not.

The Japs in the city crouched under any shelter they could find and the Big Swords did the same, sometimes Japs and Big Swords together. It seemed like a million years to all caught in it before it stopped suddenly and the sun came out.

There were two feet of water covering the cleared space between the city and the hills, rushing towards the river which was already over its banks. The Jap guns in the hills were out of commission, temporarily at least, some of them washed down into gorges and ravines.

The Jap camps were a mess and a good deal of their equipment had been carried away or ruined. All in all, the "little pink toed banties" had plenty to think of besides taking a city, even if the city did hold the Big Swords and the soldiers of fortune who led them.

In the city, as the sun came out, the Japanese caught there and the Big Swords fought it out. That was all the Japs could—and wanted—to do. But they were as badly outnumbered now as the city's defenders had been outnumbered during the attack.

JIMMIE CORDIE, GRIGSBY and Carewe stood and watched the innumerable duels, sword against bayonet. Red and the Yid hung together and did not stop to count whether they faced two Japs or twenty-two. Any Japs they saw, they charged. And the hurtling charge of a two hundred and thirty pound Irishman gone berserk, a Manchu sword in his hand, plus a Yid whose hands when clinched reached below his knees, also with a sword in his hand and "damn good und mad mit dem," was not a good thing to face. The Japanese infantrymen, mostly young men, faced it through without giving back a step and did the best they could for themselves.

A Japanese officer, with five or six men, caught in an angle made by two great stones that had fallen from a temple, emptied his revolver at Red and the Yid as they came raging up. He hit both of them, the Yid in the chest, high up and Red in the left arm and shoulder. But Red was beyond caring about what hit him and the Fighting Yid, even while he was coughing blood, kept right on. They both were out to avenge the Boston Bean and they meant to keep right on doing it until they died. The Jap officer's remaining shots went wild as Red and the Yid reached him and the soldiers with him.

"Look at them," Jimmie Cordie said coldly. "Both of those apes left their guns during battle. I hope to hell and high water they both get—"

"Steady, Jimmie," Grigsby drawled. "It is the Yid and Red you are talking about, old-timer."

Jimmie Cordie turned and looked at Grigsby through narrowed eyes. Then he laughed. "That's right, George. They are—the Yid and Red. I'll reverse the English on that hope. I hope to hell and high water they both get through playing with swords unhurt. But they are due for a—"

"I say! There goes Red down and—the Yid on top of him!" interrupted Carewe, as he started for the angle. He did not beat Jimmie Cordie and Grigsby there by a foot and he was a much lighter man.

The duelling was over in another half an hour. There were no Japanese left to carry it on. Of the Big Swords there were, all told, able to fight, three hundred men. Of Hukau's Chinese, some two hundred. The Japanese had put out of commission all but two of the machine guns and all the rapid fire guns. Of the soldiers of fortune, Red and the Yid were wounded, the Yid seriously. Jimmie Cordie, Grigsby and Carewe were unhurt in any way. Tseng Wang had a bayonet hole through his right arm.

Jimmie Cordie, after Red and the Yid had been given first aid and made as comfortable as possible, asked Red, "Why did you leave your gun, Red?"

"She jammed on me, Jimmie darlin'. I was thinkin' av Beany and didn't watch the step av me."

"I see. Fair enough, old kid. Try for some sleep."

The Yid was unconscious and so could not explain why he had left his gun. The bullet that entered his chest had, as far as Jimmie and Grigsby could judge, just grazed the top of his left lung. They were both good first aid men and both had years of experience with wounds, on themselves and on others.

"That bullet is still in him," Jimmie had said when they went to work on the Yid. "Turn him over."

One thing that was always carried and guarded as if it were their mother by all the soldiers of fortune was a combination first aid and surgical kit. They could all use it, Jimmie Cordie and Grigsby with more skill than the rest. They operated on the Yid and got the bullet that was within an inch of his skin in the back as calmly and coldly, and accurately, as if they had been surgeons all their lives.

The Yid came to as they were finishing and gasped, as he lay face down on an improvised operating table. "Vot de hell do you think you are didding? Get it away from me before I—"

"Lie still, Abie," Jimmie said distinctly. "You've been shot and George and I are operating on you. Stay put, old kid Cohen."

The Fighting Yid lived up to his name right there. He spat out some blood, then said, "O.K., Jimmie. I am put."

9

NAGAYO'S THREAT

WHEN THE BEARS went out of the guardhouse after the Jap officers the Boston Bean was right behind them, not with any idea of joining them in their attempt to mop up on the Japanese army but with the hope that during the confusion he could get away.

Once outside the door he crouched and ran along the side of the building. As he cleared it, two Japanese soldiers running to get into the fight bumped into him. The Boston Bean knew what it was all about, who he was and what he was trying to do. The two little Japs, just arrived from outpost duty, did not know any of the whys and wherefores. So the Bean had a decided edge on them. He kicked at one and landed in a place that made the Jap forget all about any desire to find out why bears were in camp.

The other Jap was too surprised to get into any position of defense and the Bean knocked him out by a right upper-cut to the point of the jaw.

Then the Bean ran for the river. More Japs were coming up from all sides and the Bean found himself more or less in the same class as a football player with the ball trying to get through the opposing team without any interference to clear the way for him. One advantage he had was that the

Japs coming up, like the two he had put out of commission, had no idea who he was or what he was trying to do. All they knew was that something hard bumped into them and was gone.

His luck held until he reached the river bank and then a flare was lighted that showed him up as plainly as if it were high noon.

The Bean was getting set to dive into the water when the light came. Before he could, three or four Japs loosed off at him with their rifles.

He straightened up, whirled around once or twice, let out an unearthly screech and fell into the river all spraddled out.

Soldiers ran up and stood on the bank, their rifles ready, waiting for some noise to fire at, but none came.

"He is dead and floating downstream," one of them said at last.

"Who was he?" another asked.

"I do not know. He looked like an Afghan."

In the morning several Japanese officers stood lined up in front of Colonel Nagayo.

"Yes, sir, I am sure it was Captain Winthrop, who was known as the Boston Bean," the lieutenant who had recognized the Bean said positively.

"And your men are equally as sure that they killed him at the river bank, captain?" Colonel Nagayo asked a captain.

"Yes, sir. Four of them fired point blank at him. He screamed, whirled around, then fell into the river and sank as a stone sinks." The captain, through his men, wanted credit for killing one of the soldiers of fortune and so stretched it a little.

"Why did they not recover the body?"

"They tried to, colonel, diving for it several times and as soon as I came up I sent out boats searching the banks for it on either side. But it had either lodged in a deep hole or the current had carried it below where the search ended."

"You brought the bear skins?"

"As you ordered, colonel."

"You may return to your commands."

The officer saluted and filed out, glad to get out of the sight of the intelligence colonel who could, if he wished, have any of them detailed to him for special duty—and the Jap officers detailed on that kind of duty to Colonel Nagayo seldom came back to their regiments.

AFTER THE OPERATION on the Yid, Jimmie Cordie and Grigsby went up on the north wall to get some fresh air.

"The Yid has certainly got plenty of what it takes," Jimmie said. "He never even let out one yelp and it must have hurt like blazes."

"That's right, Jimmie. If infection does not set in he has a fair chance of getting well."

Jimmie Cordie looked around at the hills and the river, then at Grigsby and laughed.

"Did you say a fair chance, George? They ought to be starting the last act pretty soon."

"You find the wait between acts tiresome, don't you, Jeems?"

"Yeah, I always did. I wish we could get the women and kids out of here some way. If we could I'd sit and wait for Misto Jap with a song in my heart. The way we've mussed him up won't make him any too gentle when he gets to them."

"If wishes were horses, beggars might ride, old timer. All we can do is to stand them off as long as we can and after that—who knows?"

"That's her, George. As a rescue column we turned out to be a fine lot of one-armed paper hangers. If there had been half an ounce of brains in the entire outfit we wouldn't have got caught like rats in a trap. We should have tried to hold them in the open until Hukau made the hills."

Grigsby smiled. "That is the first time I ever heard you talk about water that has passed under the bridge, Jimmie. What's the matter?"

"I don't know. I guess it is the combination of the Codfish and the women and children."

"What is written—is written. The Nine Red Gods decided against us in the matter of the Bean, and for us in the Tartar thing and the cloudburst. Another hour and the Japs would have mopped up. As it is we are still on our feet and we hold the city, and not a woman or child has been harmed."

"Well, I hope the Red Gods also decide the next round in our favor. I think the best thing we can do is to plug up all but one underground entrance and hold it as long as we can. It's a cinch we can't hold Misto Jap out of the city. Let's go and see— There goes a flag of truce up. See it? Over to the left in front of that clump of timber."

The flag of truce was answered by one from the wall above the city gates. Jimmie Cordie and Grigsby stepped outside the gates and waited. They saw a Japanese officer advance through the mud and water that was still on the ground between the city and the hills on that side.

He was followed by two soldiers who carried burdens on their backs.

"It's Colonel Nagayo," Jimmie announced. "He's bringing us the bear skins."

The Japanese colonel halted about three feet away from the two soldiers of fortune who stood there looking at him out of calm, impassive eyes. He neither saluted nor bowed. The men put the skins on the ground. "I bring to you, Captain Cordie, the skins of two bears. Also the news that Captain John Cabot Winthrop is dead."

"Thank you for the bear skins, colonel," Jimmie answered smoothly. "It is sad news you bring us regarding Captain Winthrop. We heard the bear fight last night and so have been more or less prepared for the news regarding Captain Winthrop. Why did you not also bring us his body? And—have you seen any Uryankhes Tartars around?"

"I am keeping it as, shall I say, Exhibit A," the Japanese colonel lied calmly, ignoring the question about the Tartars. "I hope very soon to have Exhibits B, C, D, E and F, to go with it. Then I will return to Tsitsihar and show all of the exhibits to some people who will be much interested in them."

JIMMIE CORDIE SMILED. "There is an old saying in my country, Colonel Nagayo, 'Catch your rabbit before you cook him.' If there's anything else you wish to tell—or ask us?"

"I have brought you the skins and the news about Captain Winthrop to show you that it is impossible for you to get word to the Big Swords or any one else who might be foolish enough to try and rescue you."

"And now that we have been fully convinced of that, what?"

"This. If you wish, you may surrender. You, Major Grigsby, Captains Dolan, Cohen and Carewe. Because you, Captain Cordie, refrained from killing me once I will see to it that you get a fair trial at Tsitsihar."

"I am afraid our ideas of what constitutes a fair trial are far apart, colonel. Let us say we surrender. How about the Big Swords in the city?"

"They will be executed to the last man."

"And the Lord Hukau and his people?"

"They will be lessoned and afterwards, those that are still alive will be permitted to go where they choose."

"And all we get for deserting them is a fair trial at Tsitsihar. I'm afraid your bribe isn't attractive enough, colonel. Can't you raise it a notch or two? Say, we get a verdict of not guilty and commissions of lieutenant general in the Japanese army—and five millions in gold."

Colonel Nagayo's face became white as he struggled to restrain his temper. "You jest, Captain Cordie. You jest, knowing that you are within—"

"It's an old Yank custom, colonel. I think that we, the exhibits B, C, D, E and F, will stay right where we are and get our lesson with the Lord Hukau and his people. Send the teachers any time, colonel. And, please try to arrange matters so that you can come with them. I would like to get you lined up with my sights before the lesson starts."

"I will come, Captain Cordie. I—I—" he snarled an order to the two soldiers, turned on his heel, and literally ran for the hills followed by the two men.

"You got him all fussed up, Jeems," Grigsby said with a grin.

"I tried to," Jimmie answered.

10

THE HIDDEN SHAFT

RED SLOWLY MADE his way along until he found Carewe, who was talking to Tseng Wang.

"Come wid me, Carewe," he coaxed. "I want to go below and see the menagerie." His arm and shoulder were bandaged.

Carewe excused himself to Tseng Wang and tucked a hand under Red's good shoulder. "Right, old dear. Carry on."

Red, once below, did not seem to be able to find anything that amused him for more than a minute or two and Carewe was just on the point of suggesting that Red get back to his bed when they came to the entrance of quite a large room, lighted by candles. In the room, around a table, sat four of the temple priests. On the table was a teapot and cups and saucers and little Chinese cakes. Red was fond of the cakes if he was not of the tea. His face lighted up.

The priests rose and bowed as Red and Carewe entered and one of them said something, gesturing towards two unoccupied chairs. He spoke in Chinese which neither Red nor Carewe understood but any one could have understood the gesture. It was an invitation to sit down and join them at tea.

"I don't understand the lingo av ye," Red said as he sat down and reached for a cake, "but I'll join ye just the same."

The priests smiled and nodded and one of them placed the cakes nearer Red and another put cups and saucers in front of them both, then slid the teapot over to where they could reach it.

"I don't want none av that stuff," Red growled. "Have ye no wine or brandy?"

"Oh, I say, old chap. We're guests and mustn't have them thinking we don't know the rules of—"

"To hell wid all rules. I want— I beg the pardon av ye, Carewe, and av them. Pour me some av the damn—av the fine tea and I'll be drinkin' it to their health. Since Beany went I'm like a dog wid the distemper. I know better, Carewe. Sure the Dolans was kings wance in Ireland wid grand palaces to live in. Manners was taught the young scuts av the family by—by— I can't go on wid it. All I am is Red Dolan and Beany is gone and the Yid is like to go any minute, and, what the hell is keepin' ye from pourin' me tea?"

"She's poured, old topper. I say, Red, tighten your belt a hole or two. We have to carry on, you know."

"Am I not doin' it as a Dolan should? Me and Jimmie and ye and—"

The Japanese guns opened fire.

The priests, Red and Carewe listened for a moment, then Red said, " 'Tis a fine thing to have to stay down here and listen to that widout a chance to answer back at all, at all. Why the hell don't they come and fight it out, man to man?"

"They'll be along sooner or later, Red. We better be

getting back—" A Jap shell came through the roof, hit a corner and exploded. It was a three inch shell that landed in the city at just the right angle to go through a small hole in the roof.

Red and Carewe, being veterans, reacted instantly as the shell came through the roof. They fell sideways from their chairs and rolled to the wall.

The priests sat where they were and were killed by shell fragments. Red and Carewe were not made safe by what they had done but it helped their chances and neither of them was hit.

Red got to his feet, his shoulder and arm hurting him badly, and started an oration that took in all branches of the Japanese army and the artillery in particular.

CAREWE TOOK THE fall, roll and escape from hurt in silence. He got to his feet and started over to the bodies of the priests to see if any of them was alive. About half way he halted. "I say, Red, look what the giddy old shell did. It blew the wall down and opened up another room. There is a shaft in it. The cribbing comes up beyond the floor and—"

"What the hell do I care about shafts wid cribbin' or widout cribbin'?" Red demanded, feeling gingerly of his arm. "The arm av me is—keep away from it, Carewe. Maybe it will cave under ye and—wait, ye little divil, I'll go wid ye."

They walked over to the shaft and looked down it. There was a rusty iron ladder attached to one side.

"Maybeso it's where the Chink keeps the treasure av him," Red said. "I wonder how far down she goes."

The War Lord Hukau came into the other room. He had heard the noise of the exploding shell and had come to see

what damage it had done. With him were two of his officers. He saw Red and Carewe and came over to the shaft.

"Do you know of this shaft, Lord Hukau?" Carewe asked
in Pushtu.

"No, Captain Carewe. I have never heard of it or seen it
before. It may be a deep well dug by some of my mother's
ancestors many years ago."

"I say, let's go down and see where it leads to," Carewe
said. "Come with me, Lord Hukau. Red, you had better
stay here, the air may be bad."

"I will like hell. If ye go I go, Carewe."

Hukau did not evince any great readiness to go down
the shaft. Neither did the officers who were with him. "It
may be," he said, "that the hole and what it leads to are
guarded by the spirits of those who dug it. I—I do not wish
to meet spirits in a dark hole and—it is not because I am
afraid but because I do not wish to offend them." It was
plain to be seen that he was very much afraid and so were
the officers with him.

"Come on with us," Red answered, scornfully. "We'll
protect you against all the spirits there are in the hole."

"Who can protect even himself against the spirits?
You think I, Hukau, am afraid? Lead the way then; I will
follow."

CAREWE FELT SORRY for him, knowing how much the
Chinese dreaded going into a strange hole in the ground
of any kind. If they knew who dug it and for what, it was
different, but any strange hole might hold something that
was guarded by evil spirits and no Chinese cares anything
about meeting spirits, evil or otherwise.

"I know you are not afraid, leader of many brave soldiers,"

Carewe said. "It is that you do not feel worthy of meeting the spirits who may guard this hole. Stay here and Captain Dolan and I will go down and see to where the hole leads and report to you."

"That will be best," Hukau answered, much relieved. "You and Captain Dolan being of another race, are far superior to all spirits. I will await your report here."

They started down and the ladder, in spite of its rusty look, held firmly. Twenty feet below the cellar the shaft ended and a tunnel started from the north side.

They played their flashlights into the tunnel for a moment, then Red said, "Look how she's timbered, Carewe. Whoever did that knows how to hold ground."

"My word, I should say so. Let's carry on."

They walked along the tunnel for fully half a mile before Carewe said, "I say, we must be right under the jolly old Japs, right now."

"If we had plenty av ammunition and the bunch av us was all here wid the Brownings I'd wish she opened up in the middle av the little scuts. But Beany is gone and the Yid is about to—come on, what are ye waitin' for?"

They went at least another half mile and then came to a shaft that also had a ladder in it.

Their flashlights showed that about fifteen feet up there was some kind of a covering over the shaft.

"Well, up we go," Red said. "Let me go first this time. I'll see what I can do about opening the damn thing."

"Red, listen, old top, your shoulder and arm are in no condition to do any shoving. Let me go first. Whatever it is may not be secured."

"I have enough left to do what I have to do," Red

answered, "shoulder or no shoulder, me bucko. Go ahead if ye want to. If ye can't move it maybe I can."

Carewe climbed up and pushed against the cover with his right hand. It gave readily, falling back like a trap door.

"It opened, Red," he called back. "Come on up."

"What do ye think I'm doin', stayin' down to make tea?" Red grunted. His wounds had made him more or less like a grizzly with the toothache.

The shaft opened in the rear room of a little stone temple that was hidden on three sides by ridges. And close to it ran the main pass leading into the mountains.

"HOLY MACKINAW!" RED said as he looked out of a slit in the wall. " 'Tis far beyond the lines av the little scuts we are, Carewe. Let's go back and tell Jimmie."

"Go first, Red. I'll put the cover back in place," Carewe answered.

They went back through the tunnel as far as the shaft. Red, who was a little ahead, halted as his flashlight played on an uneven wall of rock that filled the shaft from the floor to the roof of the tunnel.

"What the hell now?" he demanded. "Has it caved in on us? The damn thing was—look, Carewe!"

The head of a man protruded from under a big rock and close beside it the legs of another man showed. A foot or so away an arm stuck out between two jagged slabs of stone.

"I see, Red," Carewe answered, quietly. "It is Hukau and his two officers."

"They must have been comin' down when she caved in on them. How the hell are we—"

"The shaft did not cave, Red. Those slabs of stone are from the wall of the room. Hukau and his officers were killed and thrown down and then the rock piled on top of them."

"What? 'Tis right ye are, Carewe. I can see it now by the way the rocks lie. Who would do that? 'Tis a fine thing to happen when we—Carewe, how are we to get out?"

"I don't know, Red. If the rocks go all the way up I don't think we are going to get out, this way. Have you a knife on you, by any chance?"

"I have. Ye want it?"

"Yes. I may be able to cut a roof timber away and use it for a pry. We may be able to pry out some of the rocks. If the rest settle down and we can get them out one by one, we—"

"Here's the knife. Go and get the pry. I'll try to move this wan at the corner."

Red couldn't budge the rock and neither could Carewe get any results from the pry. Finally he put it down. "No use, Red. We are just using up our strength."

" 'Tis a fine jam to be in. Here we are in a tunnel leadin' to the hills and Jimmie up above not knowin' anything about it. Bad luck to the misbegotten scuts that killed the Chinks and filled—"

"There is only one way I know of to get back, Red," Carewe interrupted, "and that is to go back to the temple, wait until dark and then try to run the Jap lines. The four Manchus tried it and failed, the Boston Bean tried it and failed, now we'll try it. If one of us gets through Jimmie can open this shaft up and take the—"

" 'Tis right ye are, Carewe. Come on."

"No hurry, Red. We can't make the try before dark. I say, who could have killed Hukau and—"

"If I knew I'd tell ye but I don't any more than ye do. Come on, Carewe. The air is better up at the temple. Down here I can hardly breathe."

"All right, Red, let's go."

11

CAREWE'S DASH

THEY WENT BACK to the shrine and after closing the exit with the cover found a place close to the roof of the temple where they could see over some of the country without being seen.

"How dark has it got to be before we start?" Red demanded impatiently after a little while.

"As black as we think it is going to get, old dear. See those Jap guns down there? No—to your left on that rock ledge. Look directly over them. What do you see?"

"I don't see nawthin'. What do ye see, Mister Eagle-Eye?"

Carewe turned and looked at Red. "I say, old bean, are you all right?" Red's face was flushed and his eyes looked like two burnt holes in a blanket.

"I am. The shoulder and arm av me is raisin' hell and I feel hot but I'm all right. Get on wid it. What do ye see? How many times have I to ask ye?"

"I see water coming down one of the ravines bringing trees and whatnot with it. The cloudburst must have—"

"I see it now meself."

"Well, the water is going down to the—"

"Speaking av water, I wish I had a drink av ice-water. 'Tis burnin' up I am inside."

"Stay here and take it easy. I'll see if I can find some, old topper."

He found a well just back of the temple and in the temple a stone bowl in front of one of the idols. He rinsed the bowl out several times, then filled it and brought it to Red.

" 'Tis what I wanted," Red said after he had taken a long drink. "Pour the rest over me. 'Tis a good man ye are of the inches av ye, Carewe. I feel better already. By night I'll be as good as new."

But by night Red Dolan was not as good as new. He was decidedly the worse for wear. His fever was raging and his entire side and arm felt, as he said to Carewe, "like somewan was using the shoulder and arm av me to build fires in."

CAREWE KNEW THAT Red could no more try to run the Japanese lines with any chance of success than he could take a running hop, skip and a jump from where he was and land in the city. And, as it grew dark, he started in to convince Red of that fact.

Finally Red said, "Go on wid ye, then. I'll stay here. But, if by daylight Jimmie does not come through the tunnel, I'll know ye have failed and then, by all the saints above, I'll start meself."

"Right. I'll leave you plenty of water and—"

"Leave it and be gone. Ye talk too damn much—all the time. Who the hell do ye think— I'm sorry, Carewe. Ye know how much I think av ye. Go on, ye little cock av the world. Ye can make it. Don't think av me at all. Think av the little golden wans and av Jimmie."

Carewe got the water for Red and did what he could to make him comfortable, which wasn't much.

As he started, Red said, "I have nawthin' on me to stand off any scuts that might come. The gat av me is on me bed far back in the city."

Carewe took off his belt from which hung a holstered .45 Colt.

"I'll leave mine with you, Red."

"Will ye not need it?"

Carewe smiled. "If I'm caught, Red, a .45 Colt could not clear the way for me. Good-by, old-timer. Easy does it, remember."

"Good-by, Carewe. Good luck to ye. If ye don't make it, I'll try it—and if I don't make it, 'tis joining the Codfish we'll—what the hell are ye standin' around for? Go on about the business av ye."

Carewe, as soon as he got outside the temple, stood still for a moment. It was pitch dark, a darkness that seemed to be as thick as a London fog. Carewe like most flyers, could orient himself. He stood there and in his brain drew a straight line to the Jap guns and from them to the water in the ravine. Then he started for the guns.

"MISTO JAP MUST be taking time out," Jimmie Cordie said about four o'clock in the morning as he sat with Grigsby and Tseng Wang on the wall near the largest breach.

"He probably has enough to do getting back in shape. The cloudburst must have wrecked him more or less. The Yid says that he intends getting up very shortly."

"Yeah? Well, what Mr. Cohen says and what Mr. Cohen will do, are horses of two—"

Tseng Wang rose. "One comes," he said softly, "through the mud and water."

Jimmie Cordie and Grigsby also rose and Jimmie answered, "Your ears must be more than—I hear it now. Whoever it is, is trying for this breach in the wall."

"He is close," Tseng Wang announced a minute afterwards, and he drew his sword.

Both Jimmie Cordie and George Grigsby drew their Colts and then, with their left hands, their flashlights. "Put it on him, George," Jimmie commanded a moment later.

Two flashlights picked up a running figure about fifty feet away. "It's a—for the love of Mike! It's Carewe! How the heck did he get out and—come on, Jonathan, old kid."

Carewe came on, and when he arrived, sat down on a rock and gasped for breath.

"Red and I—Red and I went down—my word, I can't—get the giddy—old breath."

"Take your time," Jimmie answered. "Draw a long one and hold it for a minute. That will ease you up."

"I'm all right now. Red and I—"

"Where is Red?"

"Holed up in a temple way up in the hills."

"Wounded?"

"Not any more than he was, Jimmie. We—yesterday—we went...."

It took Carewe some time to tell it all. He had got to the Jap guns without meeting or hearing anything. He couldn't see anything and neither could any one else outside of the light cast by a camp fire or flashlight. Around the guns were the tents of the artillerymen and several fires. He had gone to the left, then swung back on his line for the ravine.

As he cleared some scrub timber he could see other camp fires along the ravine on both sides. He headed to the right and got well above them, and then turned left again and reached the water. There was an uprooted tree grounded on the bank. He got in among the branches and pushed it out into the water. To hear him tell it, that was all there was to it. Duck soup all the way.

The tree floated down, grounding every now and then. He would push it off, and as he said, "resume the jolly old voyage." Finally the tree floated out of the hills and grounded for good where the water became shallow. From there he had started for the city and made it, on foot.

"Well," Jimmie Cordie said, "there is only one explanation. The god of luck had tight hold of your hand, Jonathan. Tseng Wang, detail a working party of Big Swords. We'll clear out the shaft. Just who would have such a strong interest in keeping the shaft a secret that they would kill Hukau and his officers is beyond me."

"YOU'RE IN THE wrong pew," Jimmie said a little later as he, Grigsby, Tseng Wang, Carewe and a party of Big Swords entered the room where the shell had exploded. It was lighted by many torches.

Carewe looked around, puzzled. There was no sign of a wall blown out and no dead bodies of priests. Instead there were ten live priests conducting some ceremonial in front of an altar that stretched from wall to wall. Among them the high priest.

"No, Jimmie. I am sure this is the room. Smell the h.e.?"

"That doesn't mean anything. It could have come

through any of those cracks in the—you're right, Carewe. There is a piece of the shell bedded in the wall."

"The wall was blown out where the altar is. I am sure of that, Jimmie."

"Yeah? Maybeso the priests can explain about Hukau and his officers. Tseng Wang, have that altar moved to one side."

Tseng Wang, who had been looking at the priest through cold, scornful eyes, snarled an order. To a Manchu, a Chinese priest is as a snake. Ever since the Manchus took China the intrigues of the priests caused them more trouble than anything else, and all Manchus remember it.

As some of the Big Swords advanced, the high priest held up his right hand and shrilly ordered them back. When he saw they ignored the order he whipped a sword out from under his robe and ran in front of the altar.

The rest of the priests also produced swords and ranged themselves in a line in front of the high priest.

"So that's it," Jimmie Cordie said. "Cut the way through them, Tseng Wang." He was thinking of the women and children that for some reason the priests would keep in a city that was being shelled.

The priests did not last as long as it would take to tell. They fell, dead or wounded, under Manchu swords as better swordsmen than they have fallen. The altar was moved, and behind it was the room in which was the shaft.

"They did it for some reason," Jimmie Cordie said. "See if you can persuade one of the wounded to tell you why, Tseng Wang."

Tseng Wang went over to a wounded priest, lifted him up and pinned him against the wall. "Speak, dog of a priest.

Quickly, unless you wish the death of disembowelment. Why were the Lord Hukau and his officers slain and the shaft filled with rock?"

The priest's eyes closed so that he might not see the grim face and menacing eyes of the Manchu. He stammered out something in Chinese. Tseng Wang let go of him and he fell to the floor.

"The priests built the tunnel many years ago. They intended using it if it became necessary to escape from the city, carrying with them treasure they had accumulated during many years. No war lord who held the city ever knew of the tunnel. The priests held it secret for their own use. They had decided that the time had come to escape just before the shell blew the wall down. They were afraid that the Lord Hukau would use the tunnel to get the people of the city away and they would have to go also, exposing their treasure.

"After the foreign devils had gone down into the tunnel, they slew the Lord Hukau and his officers and threw the bodies into the shaft, afterwards filling up the shaft with rocks to force the foreign devils to leave by the temple exit. They thought that the men of Nippon would surely kill the foreign devils. Later, as the men of Nippon attacked, they were going to clear the shaft and escape through it."

"I see. Leaving the women and children here and the men who were defending the city for the men of Nippon to slay. As priests they were a fine bunch of copperhead snakes. Get the shaft cleared."

The shaft was cleared and the bodies of Hukau and his officers brought up. Then Jimmie Cordie and some of the Big Swords went through and got Red.

"So he made it, did he, the little gamecock?" Red said. " 'Tis glad I am to see ye, Jimmie darlin'. The fever av me has gone down and...."

12

DISCOVERED

THE JAPANESE HELD off from any attack during the day;
why, only the Japs knew. It might have been, as Grigsby
said, that they were getting back in shape.

As soon as it became dark, an advance guard was sent
through the tunnel and then the old men, women and
children were passed along into the tunnel by strong arms.

Jimmie Cordie, with a machine gun and some of the
Big Swords, remained at the shaft mouth until every living
human being was in the tunnel or outside the shrine, then
blocked up the space where the wall had been blown out
with great rocks and went down the shaft.

There was not the slightest indication that the Japanese
were aware of what was going on. And they were not aware
of it, either, until the Nine Red Gods sat in the game again.

Two Japanese non-commissioned officers, commanding squads engaged in getting the guns back in shape and
also retrieving any camp equipment that had been washed
down to lower levels by the storm, had found a large flask
of brandy which had belonged to an officer. One of them
pocketed it, and after they had been relieved they walked
into the timber to drink in peace without having to share
their find with other non-coms.

They passed the sentries with a snarled countersign and avoided the outer patrols. At last when they thought they were far enough out they sat down, their backs to a tree, and took a drink. Being converts to the theory that half a blanket was worse than none at all, they took another.

After which they began talking of Nippon and their homes. One of them had a poetic strain in him, and very soon, after another drink, began to recite poetry. All of a sudden he got the idea that he could not recite properly while surrounded by trees. He needed wider, clearer space. The top of the hill was what he needed, he decided after another pull at the bottle.

They got to the top of the hill and the would-be poet recited poetry to his heart's content. At least, he did until the flask was empty. Then they started down, neither of them any too steady on their feet.

The Nine Red Gods must have decided to give the Japanese a round because the path the two Jap non-commissioned officers followed led to a lower ridge that ran along the main pass.

"KEEP GOING RIGHT up the pass," Jimmie ordered the Manchu in command of the vanguard. "About three miles from here you will come to a pass leading to the right. Take it and keep on going. It leads to the Mountain of the Birds. From there to the Big Sword encampment the—"

"I know the way, Captain Cordie."

"All right. Get going. If you meet attack we'll come up and—"

Two of the Chinese bearers, who were carrying part of a machine gun, dropped it. One had stumbled and let go his hold, and the other, not being prepared, let go his also to save himself from falling.

The gun part fell on a rock, making quite a noise. A split second afterwards two flashlights played on the machine gun part and then on Jimmie Cordie and the men near him. Right after the light went out and there came the sound of running feet, going down the hill.

The two Japs had gotten to the ridge and had heard the sound of marching feet.

At first they thought it was one of their regiments going into the hills for some reason. They dropped to their hands and knees and got closer to the pass. Close enough to hear the gun part drop. They played their flashlights down on the pass. What they saw sobered both of them. They got up and started down the hill as fast as they could run.

"We can catch the runners, Captain Cordie," a young Manchu officer said eagerly.

"Go and do it."

Four or five Manchus ran up the side of the pass. Before they got to the top the two Jap non-coms began shouting the alarm at the top of their voices. It was not a full minute before the Jap shouts were answered, and then there came other shouts, and right after, bugle calls.

"Tseng Wang, take with you all Big Swords but one hundred who will stay here with me. My orders to Hsai are canceled. You will start the column up the pass that leads to the left just before the pass opens to the right. It leads to the encampment of the Uryankhes Tartars, which is much nearer than the Big Swords encampment. Say to the officer you designate to command the vanguard that he is to tell Sahet Khan that I, Captain Cordie, his blood brother, ask

him to protect the old men, women and children until the
Lord Chang-Lung Liang comes for them. That he is to be
friends with the Lord Chang, for whom he knows I fight.

"You will, after the column is in the pass to the left, close
it to the little men of Nippon, and as soon as the column
has reached the upper pass and starts to descend into the
valley, that pass is also to be closed by Manchu swords of
Chi who are in the vanguard. One officer is to go with the
column. The Uryankhes will see the column as soon as it
starts down. Is that plain to you, Tseng Wang?"

"Yes, Captain Cordie, it is plain. The entrance to the pass
on the left is to be closed to the mongrels of Nippon, and
also the entrance to the upper pass. They shall be closed, O
lieutenant of the head of the House of Chi. Is it permitted
that I ask a question?"

"Yes."

"And you?"

"We will close this pass right here for as long as we can,
Tseng Wang. Captains Dolan, Carewe and Grigsby remain
here with me. You will take Captain Cohen with—"

THE YID'S LITTER had been brought up by Grigsby and
Carewe. As Jimmie said "Captain Cohen" the Yid sat up.

"Nothing diddingk," he said firmly. "Captain Cohen
stays right here mit de gang und don't go novere else."

"He does like—" Jimmie began when Grigsby interrupted. "Let him stay, Jimmie."

Jimmie Cordie laughed. "At that, why not, if he wants
to. Stick around, Abie."

"I intend to," answered the Yid with a grin. "I can shoot
it a gat if I can't take von of de guns."

"Get started, Tseng Wang. We'll fuss around with the little men of Nippon."

The Manchu saluted, ordered five of the Big Sword officers and the swordsmen they commanded to remain with Captain Cordie, then ran up the pass.

"We won't last ten minutes here, Jimmie," Grigsby said. "Let's go up the pass a little ways and see if we can find a better place."

"From what I hear we better make it snappy. Misto Jap is wide awake. Come on."

Four hundred odd yards up, the pass curved sharply to the left and the walls narrowed and became much steeper. It was evident that many years ago the pass had been the bed of a swift river. On both walls there were cut-in places, some large and some small, where the current had worn away the softer rock. The moon had come from behind the clouds, and now, as Jimmie looked at the sides, it was fairly light.

"See that place on the left?" he asked. "It was made to order for a last stand thing. We'll place the machine guns there and the swordsmen can hole up below in the smaller one. The Japs can't get at us on either side or in front until they come around the curve, and there is not much room to line up for a charge. We will get set up there and wait for Misto Jap to poke his nose around the curve. At which time we will shoot it off for him."

"I say, can't the flaming blighters get into the pass beyond us, leaving a detachment to keep us holed up?" Carewe asked.

"No, Jonathan. At least not for two days. I hunted all over this country with the Uryankhes, and as far as I know no passes lead into this one either from the left or the right except the small ones below us and those that lead to the Big Swords and the Tartar encampment. And to get to those two without coming up this one means heap plenty climbing up and down and the bridging of more than a few precipices.

"Three miles as the crow flies may mean fifty miles on foot in this man's mountains. There are passes that run parallel to this, but none that come into it except the two I've mentioned. To get above us in this pass the Japs would have to get to the pass on the left. And to get there without using this pass is some job. If we can stop them for three or four hours right here, and the Big Swords can hold them a little while at the mouth of the other passes, the column will win through."

"Sure we will stop the duck-faced scuts," Red said. "Come on, let's get up there. What are ye waiting for?"

"I was explaining the topography to our old friend, Jonathan Carewe, Mr. Dolan. Start up if you are in a hurry."

"Ye better be in a hurry yerself. Hear that below us?"

"I do—and it leads me to believe you are right about hurrying, Mr. Dolan."

THE YID, ONCE he was on the cut-in, and made comfortable with his back to the wall, demanded, "Give it to me a .30-30. I can hold it under de arm and against de rock. I am still mad at dem."

"Don't get too ambitious," Jimmie answered. "You're here, aren't you? Be content with that. The jar would open that wound of yours and you'd bleed to death, you Yid chimpanzee."

"Vot de hell difference does it make if I do? I get it a few Japs in de meanvile."

"Yeah? Well, you don't get a .30-30 just the same, and I've a darn good mind to take that .45 away from you I saw Red tuck under the blanket before we started."

"Vot? Und leave it me mit nothingk? Oi, mine persecuted race! Jimmie, you ain't got it de heart to did it. I vill be good—no foolingk. I vill just sit it here und vatch until it comes de finish."

"All right, Abie. I'll take your word for it. We won't have any time to do any first aiding, remember that, old kid Cohen."

"I wonder what is holdin' the banties," Red said. "They should be here by now. Listen to them maneuvering around below. To hear all the bugles sounding off ye'd think they was afraid of an attack themselves."

"Holy cats! You've nicked it, Red. That's what they are afraid of. Those gents that put the flashes on us only saw some Manchu swordsmen and us and part of a machine gun. I'll bet the Japs think they are due for an attack from the hills and are reforming their lines. Go down and tell them it's only us, Red, and that we're waiting for them up here."

"I will not. Let the banties find it out for themselves. I wish Beany was here."

"So do we all, Red. Well, if you won't go, old man Cordie's son Jimmie is going to cork up and get a little sleep. Wake me if the doorbell rings."

"We will, Jimmie darlin'. Who is to fight the guns?"

"Not you, you red-headed ape. You might jam yours to get a chance to jazz around with a sword. I'll fight one and

George will fight the other. Carewe will help me and you can help George. Any further questions you have to ask, Mister Dolan, ask them of my friend Mr. Grigsby."

" 'Tis a sad thing to be accused av jammin' a gun in battle. Sorry the day I hear ye say it, Jimmie Cordie. For many the long year have I been wid ye and never have ye—"

"You mean sorry the night, Mister Dolan. Well, didn't you?"

"Didn't I what?"

"You know what I mean. Didn't you jam that gun on purpose?"

"Jimmie, listen to me. Since ye ask me outright, I dunno. I was pullin' trigger and thinking av poor Bean and wishin' for a sword so that I could get to close quarters wid them that got him, and—I dunno, Jimmie darlin', maybe I did pull so fast that I knew she'd jam."

"That's coming clean, Red. If you did, you did it subconsciously, and that lets you out. Forget it, Terence Aloysius."

"I will, then. What does that—that subconscious thing mean, Jimmie darlin'?"

"Ask George to explain it. I'm going to sleep."

13

THE LAST STAND

THE JAPANESE WERE, as Red said, afraid of an attack. The two non-coms told of seeing Manchu swordsmen and other men they did not recognize and of seeing a machine gun part. The Japs jumped to the conclusion that word had got to the Big Swords or to the Tartars that they knew Jimmie Cordie was allied with. So the Japs did exactly what any other force would have done. They reformed their lines to face the hills.

No outfit, civilized or otherwise, cares about getting tangled up in the hills with hillmen. There is no room to maneuver men, and less room to quickly place guns in commanding positions. The Japs were no exception to the rule. The few times any of their regiments had got any distance into the hills, they had been badly cut up. The commanding officers knew that the Big Swords and the Tartars and other fighting tribes had only one thought when trained troops were seen in the hills, and that was, "there is food and drink for our swords."

While the Japanese were not exactly in the hills, strictly speaking, they were close enough to cause them to change their battle front as quickly as possible.

They did not have any idea at all that the men seen by

the non-coms had come from the city of Fung-hwan. And so, for at least an hour, they awaited an attack that did not come. At last they cautiously advanced a couple of regiments to flush up whoever was in the hills.

The only place they succeeded in getting contact was in the main pass. The two companies that went up the pass were suddenly greeted with machine gunfire and a Manchu sword charge. The few Japs that got back reported that the Big Swords were in force there.

This still further puzzled the Japs, as they could not figure out why the Big Swords would all be in one pass and not spread out over the hills and in the other passes. So they decided to wait until daylight before investigating further.

If Jimmie Cordie had known of that decision he could have withdrawn up the pass and been well on his way to the Uryankhes before the sun came up—but he didn't. As far as he knew the Japs might any moment come up the pass in force, so he stayed right where he was.

In the morning the ruined city was still, so still that it finally dawned on the Japs that it was deserted.

A detachment was sent to it and not long afterwards the officer in command reported that there was not a man, woman or child in the city of Fung-hwan.

"But how—how could they have come through our lines?" asked a well meaning but not very bright colonel. "They have neither planes—"

"A tunnel," snarled Colonel Nagayo, almost beside himself with rage. "A tunnel that put them beyond our lines. It is they that were seen in the pass! Not the Big Swords or the Tartars! Captain Cordie and the other mongrels think they can hold the pass against us while the Chinese escape to the Big Swords! And we wait here for a Big Sword attack. Lieutenant General Mayoro, I ask in the name of the intelligence division that the pass be taken promptly!"

A CRACK REGIMENT was sent up the pass with orders to mop up, and while doing it, take the white men prisoners if possible.

The advance company of the regiment trotted briskly up the pass until it came to the curve and started around it, then came to a halt and looked around. It was the last look for a good many of them. Two machine guns opened fire, and after a moment or so there came, as the machine guns stopped, a charge of Manchu swordsmen. The Japanese, thrown into confusion by the machine gun fire, fought as they always do, bravely. But before the second company got to within a hundred yards of the curve, the first company had ceased to exist.

The Manchu swordsmen went back to their hiding place, but not all of them. Fifteen of them had fallen.

"That's knockin' the pink toed little divils off the Christmas tree," Red announced. "We can do that all day, can't we, Jimmie?"

"Well, here is a sum in simple arithmetic for you, Mr. Dolan. If we lose fifteen Big Swords and use two hundred and fifty rounds of ammunition to stop Jap Company Number One, what number Jap company will arrive right after all the Big Swords and all the ammunition have been used up? Before you answer, take a look at the ammunition."

"I never was good at arithmetic. What the hell do I care

what the number av the company is? By now the women and childer ought to be wid the friend av ye."

"That's right, Red. They ought to be there or close to there. If we can hold Misto Jap for a little while now it's a cinch that they'll get to Uryankhes territory. The column, I mean, not the Japs."

"We know what ye mean, Jimmie. Well, what's to stop us holding the Japs for as long as we want?"

"Oi," the Yid said, "how I lofe it you, Irish bummer. Come over here und I vill smack it you on de forehead mit de kiss of respect."

"Ye will what? Jimmie, the Yid scut is gettin' better—praise to all the saints in paradise. Did ye hear what he said to me, the Hester Street gibbon? Are ye really feelin' better, Abie darlin'?"

"I am, much better. Ven company number twenty-von gets it here, I vill go down and cakevalk dem back to de mines all by myself."

Jimmie Cordie laughed. "Wait until company eighty-eight gets here, Yid. You'll have that much more strength."

"Jimmie, do you think this is the last stand av us?"

"Yeah, boy. We couldn't run now if we wanted to, and—"

"Who the hell wants to run, ye shrimp av the world? There is no run in any of us and well ye know it, Jimmie Cordie."

"Did I say there was, you big ape?"

"I seen it de Irish gonif run once," the Yid asserted. "My, how he did pick it dem up and lay dem down."

"Well, ye Yid black and white kitty! Here I was worried to the heart av me about ye, and now, now ye say I ran."

"You remember it dot time in Shanghai dot you und me

und anodder feller got it into de fan-tan house by mistake? Vere de two big Chink vomen came it at us mit de brooms? You made it de first hundred yards in nothingk flat—und de next hundred in less."

"Aw, hell, who wouldn't run from a couple of women wid brooms? 'Tis not what I mean and well ye—"

"Listen, Yid," Jimmie Cordie said, "you are doing altogether too much talking. You're liable to open that—here comes company number two!"

The Japanese companies kept right on coming and would have come two at a time if the pass had been wide enough.

And as they showed they were met with machine gunfire and then sword charges. But the swordsmen became fewer and fewer, and so did the belts of ammunition for the machine guns.

In three hours there were left of the swordsmen fifteen, and of belts for the machine guns two.

THERE WAS A lull between Jap companies for some unknown reason and during it Red said, "Think av something, Jimmie. Ye always have before."

"I only wish I could, Mister Dolan. Remember the story about the pitcher that went to the well once too often? I'm afraid I've used my thinker once too often. About all I can get as a connected thought is 'I hope the column has got to the Uryankhes Tartars by this time,' over and over again. And if it hasn't, after the Japs clean up on us they still have the Manchu swords to go through in two places. Why think of anything, Red? Do you want to live forever?"

"Sure he does," put in the Yid. "He is afraid of going to de hot place mit de rest of de Dolans."

"Here they come!" Jimmie Cordie interrupted. "Hold your swords back," to the Manchu officer. "We'll let them come right up after us this time."

The Japanese did that coming up thing, without a second's hesitation. They came up with bayonets fixed, the officers with revolvers spitting flame and lead.

But they met swords of steel and .45 Colt bullets. The machine gun stayed the upward rush for a moment or two, then several Japanese soldiers below fired at Grigsby and Carewe who were now operating it. Both men were hit and fell away from the gun.

"Did ye see that, Jimmie?" Red asked as he reloaded his Colt. "George and Carewe are gone."

"They may only be wounded, Red. Stay with it, old kid."

The Fighting Yid had in some way got to his feet. He stood, his back to the wall, using his Colt .45 and talking now as ever.

The Manchus were fighting like they always fight, to the death. Jimmie Cordie and Red Dolan stood as if on parade and shot with deadly accuracy. Rifle bullets were singing the death song close to them now.

Nearer and nearer came the bayonets of the Japanese, and as they got close, the rifle fire stopped for fear of hitting Japs.

"So long, Red," Jimmie said calmly, "I hope we both go to the same—"

The thunder of countless hoofs came to their ears and mingled with it the wild, full throated, menacing yell of Uryankhes Tartars charging home.

The Japs heard it and stopped, then turned and executed

one of their rearward movements, a very fast rearward movement indeed.

Down the pass, filling it from side to side, came the Uryankhes, led by Sahet Khan. He had brought with him ten thousand of the fiercest, most dreaded fighting men of the hills, to rescue his blood brother, Jimmie Cordie. The Uryankhes fight any and all at any and all times, and to them the Japanese, for all their guns, big and little, were small men to be slashed at and ridden over. The Jap regiment in the pass went down under Tartar swords and horses' hoofs. And the Tartars kept right on.

As Sahet Khan rode past, Red whispered. " 'Tis goofy I am, Jimmie darlin', and seein' ghosts. Beany was ridin' wid Sahet Khan. 'Tis back he has come from the land av spirits to—"

"Snap out of it, Red. That was the Codfish Duke."

"I'm just after tellin' ye it was. He looked as lifelike as—"

"Red! Come to, you idiot! The Bean escaped, you double fool! He escaped in some way and got to Sahet Khan instead of the Big Swords. You look as if—well, for Pete's sake! Listen to that! That's not Jap artillery. That's Big Sword stuff. Well—" Jimmie Cordie sat down on a rock. "As long as the Big Swords and the Uryankhes have come to take our place at the party, I guess we can sit down for a minute."

"Oi, Jimmie!" yelled the Yid. "George und Carewe both tried to get it up!"

THE JAPANESE STOOD right to it and took the charge of the Uryankhes Tartars as they take all charges. But they were spread out, and regiments were more or less in other regiments' way when it came to stopping a charge that

came out of a pass. Ten thousand Uryankhes on horse-
back, who don't care what they charge and firmly think
that if they die in battle they are more than lucky, are a lot
of Tartars to stop and the Japanese found it out up there
near the city of Fung-hwan that day.

And suddenly, from hills higher than the ones on which
Japanese guns were mounted, there came a terrific artillery fire, and in addition to that, Big Sword regiments with
fixed bayonets charged up from the river and from the east
and west and on the Jap guns.

The Bean, as soon as he could swing wide, went back
to the pass.

As he arrived, Red said, "What the hell do ye mean by
bein' alive, ye long-legged shrimp from Bosting? 'Tis hopin'
ye was dead, we all was. How dare ye be alive and kickin'?"

"I hate like the dickens to disappoint you. Mister Dolan.
Where did you get it, Yid?"

"I got a bullet in de chest. It ain't nothingk, Codfisher.
My, I am glad to see you vonce more. Never mind dot
red-headed Irish bum. He vos cryin' all de time about you."

"Well, ye Yid, monkey faced—"

"Get over here," called Jimmie. "George and Carewe are
coming back to life."

Sahet Khan and the Manchu noble Chang-Lung Liang
who led the Big Swords, were old campaigners, and soon
saw that they could not whip the Japs in the open. They
finally got their men in hand and retreated to the hills.
There the Tartars and the Big Swords snarled defiance to
the Japs and dared them to come into the hills and fight
it out.

The Japanese were quite content where they were.

Chang-Lung Liang and Sahet Khan rode up to where Jimmie Cordie was giving Grigsby and Carewe first aid. Both men had been badly but not fatally wounded.

Jimmie looked up. "The women and children, Sahet Khan?"

"They are safe, blood brother."

Chang-Lung Liang looked down at Jimmie Cordie, who was kneeling beside Carewe. "You have once more fulfilled a trust, resplendent one. Again shall the golden scroll of the House of Chi be opened and the further debt to you be engraved on the sheets."

Jimmie Cordie grinned as he answered, "I think there are quite a few other names that ought to be engraved above mine, mighty one. That of Captain Winthrop among the first."

That night the Uryankhes Tartars and the Big Swords started for their encampments, leaving a fringe of men to bluff the Japs into thinking that they still awaited attack.

It did not come, and late the next day the Japanese moved to the south—without even the bearskins to show for their loss in men and equipment.

Red rode up alongside the Boston Bean. "Jimmie says that wid care and good luck, George and Carewe will pull through, Beany. Tell me about the trip av ye to the wild men—emir av the world."

"Go talk to Mr. Cohen," the Bean answered loftily. "Us emirs don't hold no truck with red-headed apes, me good man."

Red sighed happily before he began telling just what he thought about the Codfish Duke of Massachusetts.

THE MAD MONKS

*Spies of three nations wanted those
railroad plans for Chinese Turkestan—
and so did Jimmie Cordie*

1

VALUABLE PLANS

"CHINESE," JIMMIE CORDIE announced as he looked through his glasses. "A survey party. Can you see the instruments, Zagatai?"

The young Uryankhes Tartar, son of Sahet Khan, who lay beside Jimmie Cordie on a rock ledge far up on the side of a mountain in the Thian Shan range, Sinkiang province, northwestern China, smiled as he answered, "Yes, blood brother of my father, I can see them. Now they take them to a tent—and now they begin to wrap them in cloth."

He did not need glasses to see distinctly what was going on at a camp pitched near one of the main passes. The eyes of the young chieftain were like those of an eagle.

"We're in the territory of the war lord Ning-Wu," Jimmie went on. "He must have authorized the survey. They may be his men."

"Shall we go down and ask, mighty one?" Zagatai replied, his thin, dark, proud face and fierce eyes lighting up with a smile.

That there were of the hunting party that had left the encampment of the Uryankhes the week before, less than thirty men including five officers of the Big Swords, and at least three hundred Chinese in sight at the camp, made no difference to Zagatai, aged sixteen. The Uryankhes Tartars firmly believed that they could ride over and through any men, no matter what the odds against them.

"The Big Swords are at peace with the war lord Ning-Wu," Jimmie answered. He was also thin faced, dark and black-eyed. Second in command of all Big Swords, who were fighting the Japanese in Manchukuo, the slim, wiry American, one of the most famous soldiers of fortune in the Orient, was both liked and highly respected for his fighting ability by all men who fought in the far places.

"But just why he is making a survey here is— See that, Zagatai! A fight has started and—here comes a bunch from behind that pile of camp gear to get in it. Holy Moses! It's a regular Kilkenny cat fight."

Zagatai did not know what a regular Kilkenny fight was, but he knew a fight when he saw it. He watched, his delicate nostrils flaring out a little, dancing lights coming into his eyes. A fight, and Uryankhes Tartars watching it

"Make your report!" Jimmie commanded the dying Russian.

instead of— He turned a little so as to face Jimmie Cordie. "They fight, and we remain here?"

Jimmie laughed. He knew what Zagatai meant. Sahet Khan, who ruled twenty thousand Uryankhes with an iron hand, when he detailed his favorite son to go with the hunting party, had warned Zagatai to "obey all commands given by my blood brother as my commands are obeyed." Zagatai wanted to get into the fight and if Jimmie Cordie had not been there, by now the Uryankhes would have been riding down hell for leather to do it.

"Let's wait a minute and see. There go five or six men for the horse line. They are shooting their way, and—they are Japs."

"Yes, war captain of the Big Swords. See, other men run now back of the pile—they mount. Eight, ten, twelve of them. See! The Chinese open fire!"

"The Japs jumped the Chinese for something and got it. Then the bunch that—"

"They turn to the right. We can cut them off at the river."

"I guess we'd better do it. Those birds that came from the

Some were Russian, some Japanese.

pile are Russians, unless my eyes and my glasses are both
cock-eyed. We'll ask them a few questions and then ask
the Chinese a few more."

A FATALLY WOUNDED Russian sat on the ground, his back
against a rock. On the ground near him were the bodies of
twelve men, three of them Japanese, the others Russians.

Jimmie Cordie knelt beside him. Back a little ways there
stood Zagatai, the Big Sword officers and the Uryankhes
Tartars. The hunting party did not arrive in time to cut the
fleeing men off, but did before the Russian died.

Blood trickled from his lips as he spoke. He told Jimmie
Cordie of how his party arrived to seize the survey notes,
only to find that some Japanese had beaten them to it. He
had met Jimmie once, after the war, in Hong Kong.

"… and so, they suddenly attacked the tent—of the
leader—of—the survey party. I cannot—go on. My wife
and children are—are—in Hong Kong. I ask that you
take—care of them, Captain Cordie."

"I will take care of your wife and family, Colonel
Radischev," Jimmie said distinctly. "Hold fast and tell me
what has happened. You are an officer and a gentleman—
hold fast and tell me."

"The Chinese have made a—survey of the passes for
the—war lord here. I am—I am—"

"Attention!" Jimmie Cordie rasped. "Make your report,
Colonel Radischev. The Chinese have made a survey—for
what?"

"For—for a railroad, excellency."

"The Japanese came to seize it and you did the same for
the Soviet?"

"Yes. I am—a Russian. Your country—is friend of mine

now.—Don't let—my enemies keep it—promise me, Captain Cordie—I gave my life for it—save it—" The head of the Russian, who had once commanded a regiment in the War, fell forward as his spirit left his body.

THREE JAPANESE INTELLIGENCE officers rode swiftly through the hills toward the south. One of them carried, under his tunic, a red leather case, about four inches wide by ten or eleven long.

Inside the case were the complete survey notes for a single track railroad from Jarkent on the Siberian side to Saram-por on the Chinese Turkestan side.

"We win through, major," one of them said as their horses splashed through a little stream. "The Chinese did all the work—and now we have the survey."

The officer addressed smiled. "And also we have the satisfaction of having sent quite a few of the Red mongrels to hell. That alone—"

They pulled up their horses as they reached the bank. In front of them, not a hundred feet away, there had risen Chinese infantry. On the left and right and to their rear troops also showed.

The Japanese major cursed softly under his breath and as the young lieutenant's hand went to revolver butt, said, "No. Take your hand away, Lieutenant Morioka. Resistance is useless. It may be a chance encounter."

From the troops in front a girl had ridden forward, accompanied by two Chinese officers. She was slender and beautiful, dressed in immaculate whipcord riding trousers, white flannel shirt, brown leather riding boots and little white felt hat perched jauntily on her sleek young head. Her eyes were hyacinth blue, her hair bronzed gold, her skin a rich creamy white. Elizabeth Montague, special agent for war lords and potentates, patrician Englishwoman from the top of her head to the tips of her little white toes.

The three Japanese officers sat their horses, their faces impassive as the girl and the Chinese officers trotted briskly up. The eyes of the major tightened a little as the girl and her escort came closer. He had heard of the English girl who had outplayed many intelligence men.

"Who are you?" she demanded curtly, after she reined her horse to a halt within a few feet of the Japanese.

She spoke in Chinese, but before Major Osaka could answer, laughed and went on, in English, "Oh, I see. Japanese."

"That is correct," Major Osaka answered in English. "We are Japanese— And you?"

"I am Elizabeth Montague, agent of the Lord of Sin-hsai-tung." She turned to the Chinese officers. "Search them."

Ten minutes later the Japanese were on their way once more, this time without the red leather case full of survey notes.

She watched them for a moment or so, then said, "They will ride for the Japanese outpost at Hami. If they win to it they will try for us at the river. We will go south for fifty miles, then east once more on the far side of the Ami hills."

To herself she added, "And soon I will sell the survey to Nippon or Soviet."

It was the correct thing to do, but in doing it, she and her escort got too close to the border of the Kara-Kara sand. And the mad priests of Kara-Kara attack any and all who do that.

2

"HOUSE OF LORDS"

THE URYANKHES AND the Big Sword officers rode fast on the trail of the Japanese, but it was twelve hours later when they pulled up their horses at the stream where Elizabeth Montague had taken the red leather case away from Major Osaka. The Japs had been mounted on fresh, fast horses and kept well ahead of those who followed.

The hoofprints of other horses were seen and after the Uryankhes had circled and reported that a large body of men had lain in ambush, Jimmie Cordie said, "Some outfit gathered them in and then turned them loose. The great question before the House of Lords is, was the red leather case taken away from them, or not?"

The "House of Lords," at the moment, consisted of the other four Big Sword officers and Zagatai. The Big Swords were all, with the exception of the Fighting Yid, men who had served in the Foreign Legion with Jimmie Cordie. The Yid, born on Hester Street, New York, and named Abraham Cohen, received his nickname in the A.E.F., where he had been first sergeant of a machine gun company.

One of them, a tall, lean, lanky man, answered Jimmie.

"Well, Jeems, there is only one way I know of to find

out. Keep on after the Japs until we catch them, and if they haven't got the said case, persuade them to tell us who has."

He was the Boston Bean, born in Boston, Massachusetts, named John Cabot Winthrop. Called anything that even remotely suggested Boston.

"Oi, vot a brilliant suggestion," the Yid said. "Und if dey haven't got it, by de time ve find it out, whoever has is all de vay to de Rock Candy Mountains. Tell you vot, Jimmie. Send it some of de Uryankhes after de Japs und ve vill follow de—"

Some twenty-odd Chinese soldiers came out of the timber near the stream. It could be plainly seen that they were two-thirds scared to death as well as wholly exhausted. They saw the dreaded Uryankhes, turned as if to go back into the timber, hesitated as if trying to choose between two evils, and then halted.

"Shall we bring them to you?" Zagatai asked eagerly.

"If they saw Uryankhes riding toward them their hearts would stop beating. You and I will go to them, son of my blood brother," Jimmie answered.

There was an old officer with the Chinese who could speak a little English. He did not care at all for the close proximity of a Uryankhes, but Jimmie Cordie's friendly, clean-cut, Anglo-Saxon face reassured him.

The story he told was disconnected and took a long time to tell. The gist of it was that Elizabeth Montague, the golden one, had taken from some Japanese a red leather case and then allowed the Japanese to go. The regiment had then headed south. Close to a sand waste there had come a sudden attack made by swarms of madmen, armed with swords, bows and arrows and lances.

Thousands of them, according to the officer. He had been in command of the rear guard and, by chance, close to a pass that led up into the hills. Seeing that the regiment was going to be wiped out, he started up the pass with what men he had left. The madmen came up the narrow pass after them, until darkness came. What happened to the golden one he did not know. All he knew was that he finally won clear with what men the "lesplendent war captain sees."

"You are safe now, elder brother," Jimmie said. "Take your men to the stream and rest. The city of the war lord Shen is not far from here. He is a friend of your lord and will take care of you."

AS JIMMIE AND Zagatai rode back, Jimmie translated for Zagatai what the Chinese had told.

"I have heard of the mad jackals," Zagatai said, "but thought it mostly campfire tales. We will ride back to my father. Then we of the Uryankhes will see if they can wipe us out as they have done this Chinese regiment."

"First we ride to where the fight was. It may be that the golden one told of by the Chinese officer escaped in some way, as he did. Although, from what I've heard of her, she probably died right there, fighting."

Red Dolan, one of the Big Sword officers, riding beside Jimmie Cardie, asked, "Jimmie, what the hell is it all about?" From the day Red met Jimmie in the Legion, life had been greatly simplified for the big Irishman. He would ask, "What now, Jimmie?" or "How about that?" and the answer always satisfied Red.

"What is what all about?"

"The whole thing, Jimmie darlin'. What is this survey

thing ye are after and the madmen and all? Who is this girl that took the damn thing from the little midgets?"

"She is an Englishwoman, Red. I don't know such a heck of a lot about her any more than she is supposed to be one of the most clever special agents in the Orient. And, just between you and me and the tall hills on your left, I have also heard that she doesn't allow very much to stop her when she goes after anything. There have been rumors, Mr. Dolan, that more than one man has been sent on high by the fair Montague.

"The way I got it from a man who knew her is that she can outplay most men and when she can't—why, it is just too bad for the man who blocks her off, if she can make it that way. Probably there is a lot of exaggeration, Red. She may be entirely different. All I really know is that she has worked for some pretty hard-boiled war lords, generals, and what not."

"Do ye think the madmen have killed her, Jimmie?"

"Chances are they have."

"Jimmie, who are they?"

"Well, Red, I don't know very much about them, either. And nothing first hand. South of us a few miles, the Kara-Kara sands begin. All route armies, caravans, raiding parties of hillmen and other outfits keep as far away from Kara-Kara as they can, for two or three reasons.

"The commander, of the Chinese regiment and Elizabeth Montague evidently were in the same position you are, Red. They never heard about the mad priests of Kara-Kara, either."

"Any wan would think that a full regiment armed wid

guns could smack down a lot av madmen. Maybeso it was because they was Chinks."

"Your opinion of Chinese fighting ability is not very flattering, Mr. Dolan," Jimmie answered, with a grin.

"Maybeso, Jimmie. Go on wid it."

"Before I do I'll tell you that General Kai-Lun got tangled in the Kara-Kara with his route army—and only a few men came out. You will have to admit that old Kai-Lun and his route army could do some fighting."

"They could. Did the madmen get them?"

"From what I heard, the madmen did. Well, as I said, there are more things than the madmen to buck. No water, no forage, wind all the time blowing sand in your face."

"How do the madmen live there, then?"

"The mad priests of Kara-Kara live on top of a hill about in the center of the Kara-Kara. Once, many hundreds of years ago, one of the Tartar lords who had fought under Genghis Khan built a great stone city there. He—"

"What did he do for water?"

"For Pete's sake! You big red-headed ape, will you quit interrupting me?"

"Ye jump around so, ye black muzzled shrimp av the world. Tell me plain and—"

"I jump around? Go on back with the Yid and the Bean. The Yid knows about the Kara-Kara."

"That gibbon? He'd start in tellin' lies. I'm shut, Jimmie darlin'. Go ahead and tell me. Divil a time will I interrupt ye again."

"See that you don't. The Tartar lord found on top of the hill heap plenty springs. Alle same oasis, Mr. Dolan."

"How do ye know what he found?" Red asked, forgetting all about his promise.

JIMMIE CORDIE GRINNED. "I ought to know. I was there with him. In those dear, long-past days I commanded a squadron of cavalry for Genghis—"

"Will ye stop that and tell me?"

"I am telling you. Listen, Red, no foolin'. If you interrupt me once more I won't tell you a darn thing. Now—how long the mad priests have been there, how they got there, what they have to eat, or where they get it, I don't know.

"All I know is this. There are thousands of them and they are scrappers from who laid the chunk. They take on any and all and up to date no outfit that got tangled up with them has won clear."

Red studied that for a moment, then stated firmly, "I'll bet ye that the old First Regiment av the Legion could run them scuts so far off the hill that they'd never find the way back, them that was left to do it."

"No doubt about it, Mr. Dolan. But the First is far away and—"

"Jimmie, are they really madmen?"

"Depends on who is talking. They probably don't think they are at all. I guess there is no question, Red, but what they do things that class them as mad—as far as any so-called civilized people go."

"And them scuts have killed the fightin' English girl, have they? What are we goin' to do, Jimmie?"

"Find out whether they have or not, if we can. I hope she holed up somewhere. If she did, we'll take her to Shen."

"How about the thing ye are after? Will ye take it away from her?"

"First catch the rabbit. Far be it from me to take anything away from a lady. I am deeply grieved, Mr. Dolan."

"Oh, are ye? Well, she took it away from the pink-toed banties, didn't she? 'Tis only right that some wan takes it from her."

"Well, if she is still alive, you can be the one to go up to her and say, 'Hand over the red leather case, or I'll smack you out of your shoes.' She will take one look at you and hand it right over."

"What? Me? Make a threat to a woman? Double shame on ye, Jimmie Cordie, for even—"

Zagatai rode up. "There are bodies ahead in a valley. The Chinese mongrel spoke truly, mighty one."

3

CONDEMNED

THE ABBOT OF the mad priests sat in a high-backed, throne-like chair on a dais built against the south wall of what once had been a temple. He was a man of about sixty, grossly built, fat-bellied, fat-cheeked, and triple-chinned. His little, pig-like eyes slanted up at the corners, showing Chinese blood. His high cheekbones and bat-wing ears denoted some Tartar. The thick lips and splayed-out nostrils told of an African ancestor. He looked like something seen in a nightmare. And the cruel, mocking light in his eyes and the bestial smile on his lips did nothing to lessen the nightmare effect. Rather, they added to it.

Both he and his clothes, a filthy conglomeration of sheepskins and quilted cotton robes, looked as if they had never been washed.

On a table, placed about two feet in front of his chair, there rested a green jade carving. It was of three fish, each with tail in the mouth of the other, forming a circle. The bellies of the fish rested on a slab of green jade, about a foot wide and a foot and a half long. The fish were delicately and accurately carved; the eyes were emeralds.

Before the dais there crouched a Chinese boy. A little to

the left and behind him stood Elizabeth Montague. Back of her stood one of the mad priests.

She stood there, her lovely blue eyes calm and impersonal.

The English girl was in a bad jam and she knew it. Yet she stood erect and faced the abbot with absolutely no show of fear, although she thought her death by torture, unless she could find some way to kill herself, was a question of minutes.

The abbot snarled something in a tongue unknown to her and the Chinese boy translated.

"The all-powerful one says that you are not Chinese. Who are you?"

"I am English," Elizabeth answered.

That did not mean anything to the abbot and after staring at her for a moment he spoke again.

"The mighty ruler of the world say that soon you will dance on the hot stones so that three sacred ones may be pleased."

In the few short hours she had been in the captive pen, Elizabeth had seen other captives dragged out of it—men, women and children—and then heard agonized screams and wails for mercy that lasted a long time. But she answered, contemptuously:

"Tell him I am not afraid of him and that I will not dance anywhere on anything to please the three sacred ones or any one else. My friends will pay him much gold for me—and if anything happens to me they will slay him and all his priests."

The Chinese boy had no intention whatsoever of repeating what she said to the abbot. He was afraid that if he did, a whip might curl around his body which was still sore from the last whipping he had received. So he translated that the maiden bowed to the abbot in all things and would dance whenever the abbot desired her to do it.

The abbot listened, then grunted a few words.

The mad priest behind Elizabeth touched her on the arm. She turned and walked back to the captive pen, her head still high.

Inside the stone walls that enclosed about two acres of ground there were two hundred-odd huts, or hovels. They were made of wood, stone, hides and anything else that could be used on sides and roof. The mad priests evidently had trade relations with some tribe near the sands, for there were sides of boxes and burlap bags that bore Chinese and Persian markings. What the priests traded for foodstuffs there was no way of knowing. It may be that they had found the treasure of the old Tartar lord who had ridden with Genghis Khan.

ELIZABETH HAD BEEN literally tossed into one of them and a little later had been searched by two old hags. The search was for anything she could kill herself with. Her clothes the Oriental women scorned, hence did not take. The red leather case was opened and, after it was seen to contain only papers, tossed into a corner.

The hovels were filthy inside, so Elizabeth walked over toward the south wall and sat down on a bowlder. There were a good many other women, as well as men and children, sitting or standing around, waiting for the mad priests to come for them.

As long as Elizabeth had been there she had seen no

food brought in and most of the faces of the captives were gray with fear and starvation.

She had been in tight places before and gotten out. But this time there was no out she could figure—except one. That she should escape from the mad priests and make her way across the sand to the hills and once in them win through to a friendly war lord, weaponless and alone, was not within the bounds of possibility—and she knew it.

There was only one thing she could do, and that was to get close to one of the mad priests and try for his sword or dagger. Once she had it—she smiled a little as the thought came to her—she would do what dancing was required somewhere else than on earth.

As she smiled, the sun came out from behind a cloud and a ray slanted down on the roof of her hovel. By chance she was facing so that she saw a glint of what looked like steel. She looked closer and saw that the reflection came from a piece of iron band that had been left around a box top. It was half torn off, about six inches long, sharp and jagged at the torn end.

She looked at it for a moment, then smiled again. There was no need for her to try to get close to a mad priest. She rose and sauntered carelessly over to her hovel.

THE VALLEY IN which the mad priests made their attack on the Chinese regiment escorting Elizabeth Montague was a bloody shambles of the dead. The Chinese had fought manfully to protect "the golden one," and for their lives, as the bodies of hundreds of the mad priests attested. The dead of the mad priests had been big, lean, hairy men, some of them naked to the waist, some entirely naked save for a loin cloth and some few with long black robes, black hats that looked a good deal like old fashioned women's bonnets. On the feet of those that were robed were sandals. The mad priests were not all of one race or tribe. They seemed to be a mixture of all Oriental peoples. Some looked as if they had Tartar or Manchu blood, others seemed more like Chinese, Persians or Mongols.

There were guns, swords, lances, bows and arrows scattered around everywhere. It was evident that the mad priests who survived the attack had made no attempt to pick up weapons or to bury their dead.

Near the body of the colonel of the regiment Jimmie Cordie found an empty Webley revolver, a natty little white felt hat and a riding glove. The Uryankhes had ranged the hills, and if Elizabeth Montague had escaped they would have found her.

The battlefield was searched, and at last Jimmie Cordie said, "Well, they've got her. For some unknown reason they took her alive."

"Und avay goes it de red leather case," the Yid added.

Jimmie Cordie's eyes, which usually held an amused smile, grew cold as he stared at the Yid. Finally he said, "The red leather case, Mr. Cohen, has become of secondary importance."

"Vot? Oi, Jimmie! Excuse me, I esk you. I didn't mean to—"

"All right, Abie. It's a heck of a good plan to think once in a while before speaking."

"That Yid gibbon think?" scoffed Red. "What wid? He has no brains to—"

"That will be for a little while. Let's get down to it. They have probably taken her to G.H.Q. We'll go and get her."

"Come on," said Red. "What are ye waitin' for?"

A man fully as big as Red laughed. "Let's wait a minute, Red. Jimmie, you say we are going to get her. What with? A few Uryankhes Tartars and our thirty-thirty rifles? We won't get to first base, let alone to—"

"Have I lived to see the day that ye back away from anything, George Grigsby?" demanded Red. "What do ye care how far we get?"

Grigsby, ex-Foreign Legion and major of infantry, A.E.F., known in the Orient as "a damn good man to have along," smiled at Red.

"I don't—but Miss Montague might, old-timer. I was going to suggest that we try to plan something that at least has a chance of succeeding."

"Right ye are, George. Think up something, Jimmie."

"It may take me all of three minutes, Red. George is right about our not getting to first base. To take anything away from the mad priests of Kara-Kara by force would require a—"

"Jeems," the Boston Bean interrupted, "I have just had a brilliant thought."

The Bean always looked mournful and sleepy. It was a very misleading look. The Bean was reckless, happy-go-lucky, and always wide awake.

"YEAH? WE'VE HAD experience with your brilliant thoughts, Codfish, and most of the time soon afterward we wake up in the hospital to hear the nurse say, 'Take this nice medicine.' What is this one?"

"You wrong me, Jeems. Well—"

"Wrong ye, ye Bosting beaneater? Can wan spoil a bad

egg? I'll answer me own question. They cannot. Av all the—"

"Put a jaw tackle on, you big red-headed ape. Is this the time for broadcasting? There is a girl in the hands of the mad priests and every minute counts. You know what they do to captives? They have torture down to a science. If you can't help us frame something, at least keep that big mouth of yours shut. And that goes for you, too, Yid."

"Oi, vos I sayink anythink, Jimmie?"

"No, but you looked as if you were going to. Let's have it, Bean."

"Well, the brilliant thought is—we become mad priests."

"What? Listen, Codfish. What I told Red and the Yid goes for you, also. This isn't a case of our lives being in danger. There is a girl in—"

"So you just said," the Bean answered gravely. "I'm not kidding, Jeems, me good man. We become mad priests, walk calmly across the sand, arrive at the hill in the darkness, find out where Miss Montague is held, get her and serenely walk back to the hills whistling 'God Save the King.'"

" 'Tis goofy ye are, yerself," Red said with deep conviction.

"He is, like heck. Bean, in my next army you may be a proud and haughty corporal. It was a brilliant thought that has made up for all your darn un-brilliant ones. Let's see what we can do toward becoming mad priests. We'll strap our forty-fives next to our skins and—"

"Wait," commanded Red. "Do ye mean to say that we are goin' to put on them damn robes and them bonnets and—the skins av us is white under our clothes, Jimmie.

Look at them bare legs and them little what-you-may-call-
'ems. Am I to walk across the hot sands wid them things
on the feet av me?"

"They are called sandals, Mr. Dolan. Yes, you are to walk
across the hot sands with them on your feet, and further-
more, you are going to like it."

"I am like hell. Why can't we—"

"We could, but we don't intend to. We'll send Zagatai
and the Tartars home, cache our rifles and clothes and trust
that the Nine Red Gods will play on our side."

Zagatai did not see that going home thing at all. He
wanted to stick right along, but finally Jimmie convinced
him that the Uryankhes would only add to the danger of
being discovered.

A small party could go where a larger one could not. Five
mad priests straggling along would not attract the attention that a body of twenty-odd would. Privately Jimmie
was afraid that the hot tempered Uryankhes, who held all
other tribes in contempt, would at once start a fight, irre-
spective of odds, once they were close to the mad priests.

He told Zagatai that the thing for him, Zagatai, to do
was to ride as fast as he could to the main encampment of
the Uryankhes and return with a strong column.

"Then, when we are followed from the hill, after having
rescued the golden one, the Uryankhes can drive the mad
priests back."

That pleased Zagatai, who answered, "You will see us
ride over the mad dogs, grinding their faces into the sand
with the hoofs of our horses."

4

OVER THE SAND

RED LOOKED AT the Boston Bean. "Ye know what ye look like to me? Ye look like something the cat brought in."

"Oh, do I? Have you any idea what you look like, me good man? Any self-respecting cat would take one look at you and then step around you."

"Und dot is smacking de big Irisher vare he lives," the Yid announced, as he wiped the sweat from his eyes. "Vy can't it you alvays look like a gentleman, Mistaire Dolan, like I do?"

Words failed Red. He opened his mouth to say something, could not think of anything bad enough, so contented himself with glaring at the smirking Yid.

They were then ten miles across the sands and, up to the time Red spoke, had seen nothing of the mad priests. At the battlefield the Boston Bean had acted as director and chief costumer. He ordered them back to where there was some dirt and mold, each man carrying a desert water bag of which there were plenty where the mad priests had discarded them to charge. Each man also carried a long black robe, a bonnet and a pair of sandals.

Red protested bitterly at being "all smeared up wid di-ert-ty dirt," and the possibilities of there being cooties in the robes. He was a cleanly, fastidious soul, but all his protests got him from the Bean was more dirt. All of their faces and hands were deeply bronzed and none of them carried any excess fat. Their feet were white, but not after the Bean passed them as O.K.

At last he said, "Well, I guess you'll do. Red, a little more dirt under your left eye wouldn't hurt. You look very mad, but not quite mad enough to suit me."

Red's answer to that reached new heights, even for him, and ended with, "Tend to yerself, ye long-legged cross between a Bosting jacksnipe and a black and white kitty."

"Outside of that, the red-headed ape likes me," the Bean answered. "If we don't sweat it off before we've gone a mile, we'll pass anything but a close inspection. Take the deck once more, Jeems."

They cached their clothes and rifles and horse equipment and hid the horses in a little blind cañon. Their .45 Colts with belts heavy with ammunition they wore next to their skins as suggested by Jimmie Cordie. And each of them, also at his suggestion, cut a slit in the robe so he could get at the Colt in a hurry. At the battlefield they each picked up what weapons they fancied. Red, Grigsby, the Yid and the Bean took sword and lance. Jimmie Cordie took a sword and then picked up a long bow and a quiver full of arrows.

"What are ye takin' that damn thing for?" Red demanded.

"Because, Red, I am one of the kind of archers you read about. I've always wanted to go into battle with a long bow. I can send an arrow four hundred yards with—"

"You mean by, Jeems. By express. Now, we will all take the

water bags and trip gayly on our way," the Bean announced, forgetting he had just "given the deck to Jimmie Cordie.

AS THE YID asked Red why he could not always look like a gentleman, Jimmie Cordie, who had been a little ahead with Grigsby, dropped back.

"We'll have to hit it up, gents. I've heard that the hill is about thirty miles from the border of the sands. We've gone about ten, and it's four o'clock.. If we don't arrive and do our searching and what not in the dark, we're sunk."

"Oi," the Yid mourned, "hit it up? How can ve did it, I esk you? I sink it up to de knees now mit every step." The Yid was very nearly as broad as he was long, with powerful shoulders and arms long enough for him to touch his knees with clenched fists without stooping.

Red claimed that the Yid was first cousin to—and looked like—a gorilla. And there were men in the Orient who stated they had just as soon tackle the gorilla as the Yid when he was really angry.

However, Red's statement was highly exaggerated. The Yid's face, in repose, was like the face of some Hebrew patriarch of olden days.

"THE BENIGHTED HESTER Street scut can't take it, Jimmie," Red said. "Let's carry the—"

"Vot? I can't take it? Start runnink, Jimmie. I vill show it dis—"

"You two kidders better save what energy you've got. You better dirty up your face, Yid. You've wiped off most of the camouflage. Red, you and I will set the pace."

"How far is it, Jimmie?"

"Well, if the hill is thirty miles in, and if we have gone ten, if I haven't forgotten how to subtract, it is twenty miles,

Mr. Dolan. Come on, we'll send George back to keep these two synthetic mad priests company."

"Good-by, Yid. I know ye can't keep up. Dig a hole, in the sand and cover yerself all but the nose av ye. I hope wan of the real quill comes along and steps on it for ye. We'll be seein' you on the way back."

"Take it me up dere mit, Jimmie. I vill run dis Irish bummer down to a visper."

"I bet you. Try it on the way home. I have a feeling we are going to get plenty of that running thing. Come on, Mr. Dolan. Never mind answering Mr. Cohen."

It was hard going, very hard. The wind blew continually, driving sand in their faces and eyes. It was hot and the humidity was frightful.

But they were a hard-bitten crowd, and all of them "in the pink." They needed to be to cross the Kara-Kara sands. Red walked silently beside Jimmie Cordie for a few minutes and then said, "Jimmie, tell me about the survey thing."

"What?" Jimmie had been thinking of a girl in the hands of the mad priests and had been offering up little prayers, although he was not what is known as a religious man, that they had not harmed her.

"Tell me about what the Russian had and why the little pink-toed midgets wanted it. How come if he was a Russian did he want to sell it to the Soviet?"

"Well—while we are taking a pleasant walk before supper, I'll tell you all I know, Red. It isn't much."

The Yid came up and fell in behind Jimmie.

"Vot is de idea of draggink de line dis vay? My, such

slow valkers. I vill set it de pace from now on. Take it hold of my hand, Irisher."

"What? 'Twas slow we was goin' because av ye, ye monkey-faced, flat-footed cross between a—"

"Do you want to hear the how-come?" demanded Jimmie.

"Sure I do. Wait till I put this Hester Street Yid in the proper place av him."

"That's just what I don't want to hear, Mr. Dolan. The chatter of you two chimpanzees gets on my nerves."

"Ye? Wid nerves? I never thought ye had any, Jimmie darlin'. Keep the mouth av ye shut, Abie. Jimmie is nervous."

JIMMIE LAUGHED. "NOT quite as bad as that, old kid. But right now I can do without a lot of wah-wah."

"I'm shut, Jimmie."

"All right. I'll start off. But listen: one more interruption and back to the rear you'll both go. Red, this is short and sweet, principally short. In the last, twenty years of the nineteenth century, the Russians started to build a lot of railroads. The most important at the moment is the Siberian. The first section was started from Chelyabinski to Omsk.

"A little later the Russians started to build the Pacific end from Vladivostok to Khabarovsk, which is some four hundred and seventy miles north of Vladivostok. Get that place in your head, Red. It is where the Soviet is massing troops—big and little guns—planes and what not. The Japs will try for Vladivostok and then Khabarovsk. Then they will try for Chita and Irkutsk. If they can take the last two, they have the Soviet blocked off from Manchuria and

also from Vladivostok and the North. The Chinese and the
Russians built the Chinese Eastern to—"

"Jimmie, what the hell has all this to do wid the case we
was after till we found out about the girl?"

"Everything. Here—the Soviet knows that if the Japs
can knock 'em off the Christmas tree anywhere along the
Chinese Eastern the other side of Manchuria, especially at
Omsk, Irkutsk or at Chita, they will be in a bad way, as far
as holding anything south and east of the Siberian border.
That is the reason the Soviet is double tracking the line as
fast as they can and also massing troops from Khabarovsk
to Chita. It is a case of—"

"I'll take the word av ye for it. All ye are doin' is gettin'
me all mixed up. Tell me plain."

"I'm trying to, Red. Listen. The Soviet has known for a
long time that the Japs would try to cut them off and—
holy cats! Wait until I tighten my belt. It's taking the skin
off my left side."

"Mine has taken the skin av me off both sides. Tuck the
robe av ye up and use it as a pad like I have done."

"I'll tighten it up a hole. No likee the feel of this felt or
whatever it is. Where was I?"

"Ye said that the Soviet knew that the little bamalams
would try to cut them off."

"That's right. So the Soviet, as quietly as they could do
'er, have been putting down track from Omsk to Jarkent on
the Siberian side. Now, to get into Manchuria—"

"De track is all down," the Yid stated.

"And how the hell and gone do ye know?" demanded
Red scornfully.

"Vy shouldn't it I know, Irisher? I vos dere ven dey did

it as chief engineer of de whole cheese. Dot reminds me of another song. 'Oh, I'm de chief engineer of a von shirt laundry, down on de river ba-ha—ank.' You vish to hear it de rest of de song, red-headt?"

"While you are deciding, Red, I will drop back with George and the Bean. You two double morons would make a preacher put his Bible down and—"

"Don't do it, Jimmie darlin'. I will ignore the Yid scut as a gentleman and a Dolan should. Get on wid the story."

JIMMIE CORDIE LAUGHED. "You have got me so mixed up myself that I don't know where to get on from. Maybe this will make it clear to you, Red. The Soviet wants to come through the Thian Shan with a railroad so they can come up through the Khanates if the Japs take the Chinese Eastern. By doing that, the Soviet can still unload troops in Manchuria."

"But, Jimmie, 'tis all av a thousand miles from Omsk to the Thian Shan where we are."

"I know it is—and another thousand or so through the Khanates. But two or three hundred thousand men, when they are Reds, can lay a whole lot of track in a day, Mr. Dolan. Ask Chief Engineer Cohen about it if you don't think so."

"I'll ask the Yid monkey nawthin'. Go on wid it."

"All right. The Chinese were making the survey, or rather had made it. The Japs knew about it and tried for the notes after it was finished. Some Russians did also. The Japs—"

"The Russians tried for it for the Soviet? But if they did, what did that fellow mean by tellin' ye to sell it to them? If he was van av them, is the scut sellin' out his own side?"

"There are a lot of Russians, Red, who are for Russia but

not for the Soviet. That bird was one of them. How he got the dope about the survey I don't know. Evidently he got some of his sidekickers and came up to get it, hoping to make a sale of it to the Soviet for enough to put himself and his family on Easy Street. Maybe he was going to sell it to the Japs, for all I know.

"But at the last, he wanted Russia to have it."

"Why should the little dish-faced polecats want it? They ain't buildin' a railroad too, are they?"

"No. But as long as they have it the Soviet hasn't, sabe? It takes time to make a survey through a mountain range."

"Well, why can't the Soviet or the Chinks make another?"

"They can, but in the meantime, heap plenty things can happen. The war lord Ming-kai was probably fooled into thinking the survey was for China. If I get back I'll see that he is disillusioned, by gosh. And also see that the Uryank-hes and the Altai Tartars are— Heads up! Let George and the Bean catch up with us. Here comes seven or eight of the real thing. We will let them make any play. Our game is to plod along, ignoring them."

"Sure," the Yid said with a grin, "just as if ve had known it dem for years und never did like dem anyvay. Keep it de bonnet on, Irisher. If dey see it de red-head, maybeso dere ain't no mad priest red-heads."

"And ye keep that hook nose av ye outta sight. Maybeso there ain't any mad priest Yids, either."

The Yid and Jimmie both laughed, and Jimmie said:

"That is good advice for both of you to take."

5

HAND TO HAND

THERE WERE SEVEN of the mad priests in the party that came up. Three of them with robes, sandals and bonnets. The other four were naked from the waist up. They all carried desert water bags and swords for weapons. That the mad priests had no suspicion of the little party of five that was walking doggedly along over the sand was evident by the way they came up.

"Our priestly brothers are heading for G.H.Q.," the Bean said, "the same as we are."

"Get all wah-wah out of your systems before they get here," Jimmie ordered. "No talkee at all. We're the kind of mad priests that don't speak. And, if it comes to a showdown—no gun-play. Shots might bring eight hundred and sixty more of them. We'll take them with swords."

"Don't forget the bow and arrows av ye," Red said. "Try it out on the scuts. 'Tis well widin' four hundred yards, me bucko archer."

"Steady," Grigsby warned. "They are getting close enough to see lips move."

The mad priests were all big men, and if they were maniacs or crazy men they did not show it very much. Two or three of them had a vacant, staring look in their eyes and three of the others had wild, cunning looking eyes. But there was no yelling or dancing.

One, a black robed and bonneted man, had cold blue eyes that appeared to be absolutely sane. He seemed to be the leader.

They came up on an angle and did not attempt to mix in with the party of five they had joined. The soldiers of fortune were walking now in wedge formation, not as if premeditatedly but as if by chance. Jimmie Cordie was the point, then came the Bean and Grigsby, then, just a little way out, the Yid and Red. The mad priests came up on the Yid's right, Red being to his left.

They were bunched, more or less, the leader a little ahead. When he got up to Jimmie Cordie they slacked down their pace and began plodding along also. Nothing was said and none of the mad priests looked closely at individuals of the party they had come up with.

It wasn't a place conducive to conversation anyway. The wind was blowing sand as it does a sleeting rain. All of the priests, mad and synthetic, had their heads bowed and their bodies bent forward, bucking it. Half an hour went past, an hour. And there happened what Jimmie Cordie had hoped would not happen. Red had said, "Maybeso there ain't any mad priest Yids, either." He need not have used the word "maybeso."

The bonnets they wore had attached, on either side, long streamers of the same cloth they were made of. They were patently used to tie the bonnet on by knotting under the chin. The soldiers of fortune had all done that, after they had all chased their bonnets over the sand when they first encountered the wind.

The Fighting Yid, when he began to perspire freely, loosened his. A particularly fierce gust of wind completed the job. At the identical second that it did, the mad priest nearest him turned a little to adjust a water bag. His eyes were on a direct line with the Yid. The wind lifted the bonnet from Mr. Cohen's head and it sailed away. The mad priest looked at the unmistakably Semitic face and, as he looked, let out a wild yell.

Every man, in both parties, that was ahead of him halted and turned. Two or three of the mad priests were behind him, and Red was about on a line.

The mad priest was drawing his sword as he yelled. He yelled again as he charged the Yid, who was only six feet from him.

This time he yelled, "Yehuda!"

AS THE MAN drew his sword, the Yid's right hand flashed in under the robe to the butt of his .45 Colt, then he remembered what Jimmie had said about no shots, which spoke well for the Yid's chilled steel nerves.

He did not have time to draw his sword and he knew it, so he did the next best thing. He was carrying one of the heavy water bags, made of skin with the rope over his left shoulder. His hand left the gun butt and went to the rope, his thumb going under it. His left shoulder went down and his left arm slipped out of the rope. The Yid swung the bag with all the power of his massive shoulders, straight into the face of the mad priest, who went down as if hit on the point of the jaw with a sledge hammer. Almost before he hit the sand the Yid, who was as fast as a black leopard, was on him. One hand closed around the mad priest's sword wrist, the other around his throat.

The mad priest heaved up and almost threw the Yid off. The Yid let go the sword wrist and his left hand and forearm went under the mad priest's body. There was a flurry in the sand, and then the Yid got to his feet. The mad priest was dead. What the Yid did to him, only the Yid knew, but whatever it was, it ended all things on earth for one of the mad priests of Kara-Kara.

The leader of the mad priests, thinking only of a Jew being there, turned, drew his sword and started back toward the Yid.

Jimmie Cordie was about three feet ahead of the leader, to the left. Grigsby was closer to another mad priest than he was to the leader when the leader started. The Bean, Red and Grigsby had their swords out. The other mad priests drew at once. But they were surprised, and the soldiers of fortune were not, which gave a distinct edge to the five against the seven, six now, as the Yid rose.

The leader raised the sword to cut Grigsby down as he saw Grigsby engage the mad priest close to him.

The four other mad priests were closer to Red and the Bean than to any one else. The Bean, as the Yid hurled himself at the mad priest, had turned and taken three or four running steps toward the Yid, hoping to arrive in time to block the charge. This, while the Yid was slipping his arm out of the water bag. It put him, with Red, fairly in front of the four mad priests who by now had gotten over their surprise.

Jimmie Cordie, at the point, was in the clear as far as having a foe to face. The longbow was strung and he was carrying it in his left hand. The quiver of arrows was slung over his right shoulder. He ran forward and to the right a little, about two yards. As he ran he plucked an arrow from the quiver and fitted it to the string. Jimmie Cordie was fast on his feet and his brain and muscle coordinated perfectly. He turned, raised the bow, and sent an arrow between the shoulder blades of the leader, to the feathers. He had drawn it to the head. Jimmie did not know it, but he had a Manchu bow of ten strengths, about one hundred and thirty pounds pull. That he could pull an arrow to the head told of the strength the slim, wiry Jimmie Cordie possessed.

The leader dropped his sword and fell forward. Grigsby was outmatched by the other mad priest, who threw Grigsby's blade far out to one side. The mad priest yelled in triumph and lowered his sword for an upward and inward slash. He did not live long enough to complete it. An arrow sank deep into his throat.

NOW THE ODDS had changed. It was four mad priests to five soldiers of fortune. But the four mad priests were all attacking Red and the Bean.

The Yid had put forth every ounce of strength doing what he did to the mad priest, and was staggering toward the Bean and Red to get into the fight. But he was, right then, as he told Jimmie after the fight, "as veak as a sick kitten, ain't it."

Red, running true to form, had taken a couple of steps forward to meet the two mad priests who were charging him. The Boston Bean, more cool-headed, promptly retreated a little way and began circling around. One mad priest was faster than the other of the two that came after the Bean and reached him first.

The Bean was no swordsman and never claimed to be.

But he had what the mad priest had not, a clever brain. He sank on one knee as if he had tripped. The mad priest ran in, sword up. The Bean lunged forward and the mad priest spitted himself on the Bean's sword. The Bean's long arms also had plenty of strength. The sword point was entering the priest's body before he was close enough to cut down.

Red Dolan, who was all of two hundred and thirty pounds of bone and muscle, was having the time of his life. He dearly loved a fight of any kind and a fight with swords especially appealed to him. He did not care how many swords faced him. He had "wan" for himself and the rest of it was quite all right.

He engaged both priests, roaring out insults in English, the French of the Legion, and whatever other languages he had a few words of.

The robe handicapped him a little, but he held it up in his left hand and went to work.

The mad priest that had been beaten to the Bean arrived. But a second later he joined the other on the sand. Jimmie Cordie put an arrow through the mad priest's stomach and a second later another entered his opened mouth.

The Bean looked around at Jimmie. "The next time, Jeems, me good man, keep those arrows farther out. The feathers of the last one tickled my ear."

"I intended to nick it. Look at Red waving George off! Step to the left, Codfish, you're in my line of— The Yid got one!"

The Yid had received some new strength from a reserve and in spite of Red's orders to "keep away from us, ye Yid gibbon," had, without waiting for the mad priest to turn and defend himself, started a cut from as far back as his right hand would reach. There is no question but what the Yid had, as Jimmie said, got one.

As he did, Red got the other. The priest was a better swordsman than Red; but he didn't have Red's strength and he did not have sense enough to keep away from Red until he could feint Red's sword out of position. He smashed right in and got smashed.

"And that," the Bean said, "is that. I move that from now on, Mr. Cordie's son Jeems packs a bow and arrows. One—two—three men have fallen to his trusty bow. His grandpa drew a good bow at Hastings and—"

"Get to Red! He's going down! Get him, Yid!"

Red had been reached twice by the swords of the mad priests. Once in the left shoulder and once, as he struck down the blade, in the right leg above the knee. He had been standing there, sword in hand, swaying back and forth, putting his whole heart and soul into cursing the Yid with the black curse of Cru'mel for interfering in his business.

The Yid was trying to get a word in edgeways, but not succeeding when Jimmie shouted.

THE BEAN AND the Yid both got to Red and eased him to the ground. The mad priest who had gone down coughing blood raised himself on an elbow, pointed a finger at the Yid and began to laugh. As he laughed, the blood poured out of his mouth.

It was a ghastly thing to see, but it did not last long. He stopped laughing, tried to get to his feet, failed to do it, and sank back, dead.

"Oi," the Yid said, "vot a pump dot guy's heart vos."

"Never mind about pumps. Help me get this robe off Red," Jimmie ordered.

Red's wounds were cuts, not very deep or long but deep enough to cause him to lose a lot of blood. Jimmie washed the cuts out and then bandaged them with cloth torn from a robe.

That was all he had to do it with. Whether infection would set in or not he did not know, but he had to take the chance.

"Well, we take seven priests for a buggy ride and lose one man doing it. If that proportion holds good, mad priest number thirty-six or seven is going to stand around looking for some one to fight. We'll have to pack Red. He's all right. He's only lost a little blood."

"Maybeso ve can make it a litter mit swords und vater bag skins," the Yid offered.

Two hundred and thirty-odd pounds to carry and four of them to do it. It was hard enough work packing themselves across the sands, yet they laughed as Jimmie answered, "What is the matter, Mr. Cohen? Are you getting feeble? I thought a Cohen could carry a Dolan for a few miles without any trouble. Why the 'we'?"

They made the litter by emptying all but four water bags, then cutting them. The ropes they used to bind them to sword hilts. When it was finished, it wasn't much of a litter, but it bore Red's weight after he was placed on it and it was lifted to the shoulders of Jimmie and the Yid in front, Grigsby and the Bean in the rear.

"All set?" Jimmie asked. "Let's go! *Allons, enfants perdus! Boutez en avant!* In other words, get going."

IT WAS ABOUT two o'clock in the morning when they

saw campfires on top of a big hill, about a half a mile dead ahead of them. No more mad priests had been met. Red had regained consciousness after they had packed him three miles. He sat up, nearly wrecking the litter, and demanded, "What the hell is it all about?"

Jimmie Cordie turned his head and issued a few orders to Mr. Dolan. "Get down, you red-headed ape. All the way down on your back. Put that bonnet over your head again. Stay that way until I tell you to get up. You were cut twice and have lost a lot of blood. We'll dispense with any wah-wah from you. If you want to be among those present at the hill, stay down until we reach it."

Red promptly got down, muttering, "Aw, hell, I'm all right."

Jimmie heard him and answered, "Sure you are, old-timer. You'll be a darn sigh righter if you obey orders."

Red did obey the order about getting down and keeping the bonnet over his head, but he kept up a continual grumbling, to which no one paid the slightest attention. Before the hill was sighted there was plenty to occupy their attention besides Red Dolan's broadcasting. Among other things, whether they could stick it or not. The loose sand, the heat, the humidity, the wind blowing sand into their faces, the black robes, the sandals, the belts heavy with ammunition against their naked skins, for a few of the other things.

"Well, we've made it within sight of G.H.Q., anyway," Jimmie said. "Put Mr. Dolan down for a moment or so. Easy does it. Hold your end up, Yid, until we get down to you. Fine. Now—"

Red sat up, tossing the bonnet away from him. "Jimmie, I been thinkin' of it. Where did ye learn to shoot a bow?"

"Well, for Pete's sake! What a time to begin asking questions. I was taught how to shoot a bow, Mr. Dolan, by the Uryankhes Tartars. Now you know all about it. How do you feel?"

"I'm all right, Jimmie. The cuts av me are all healed and I feel O.K. Wait, now, I'll get up and show ye."

"No. Sit there until we start up the hill. Those cuts are not healed, you idjut. George, I think we better leave Red here with one of us and—"

"What? Leave me here? Ye will not, Jimmie Cordie! As weak as I am, I'm a damn sight better man than any av ye. Start up the hill and see."

"Not so good, Jimmie," Grigsby said. "That would entail our coming back this way—and the chances are that we are not coming back any way. If we left a man with Red it would weaken us just that much and—"

"My idea, George, is that three men can do just as much as five can. If we are uncovered, it will only take the mad priests just a little less time to mop up on three than it would on five. If we pull it off, we can come down the hill in this direction as well as any other."

"That is right, Jeems," the Bean answered. "Very much so. But I think, if Red can make it up the hill—wait a minute—why not continue to pack him up?"

"Because, if the mad priests do not take care of their wounded and sick, it would draw attention to us that would be fatal."

Red got to his feet. "Listen to me, Jimmie Cordie. When I met ye in the Legion 'twas durin' a fight wid the black-hearted scuts av the Bat d'Af we was havin' in the café, wasn't it? It was. Ye fought by the side av me then. That's many long years ago and still we do be fightin' side by side. I ask ye to remember the while I ask ye this, all foolin' to wan side. Are ye goin' up that hill widout Red Dolan by the side av ye, weak though he is? I can still pull the trigger av me forty-five, and—"

Jimmie Cordie laughed. "Come right along, Mr. Dolan. I hope that trigger pulling will not be necessary. But get this—I want you to take it as easy as you can, at least until your strength comes back."

"I will, Jimmie darlin'. Come on."

"All right, we will. I'll say this, before we start. About that side by side thing. I've always been glad you were beside me, you big Irish, brick-topped wild man from Cork."

"The same to ye," Red answered happily as he fell in beside Jimmie.

6

INVASION

THE RUINS OF the stone city covered a large space. There were piles of stone that once had been proud temples. Palaces half in ruins, street after street of what had once been stone houses, two stories high. Barracks, audience halls, warehouses, stone fountains from which there still gushed clear, cold water, squares and courtyards and artificial lakes and little ponds, all mixed together and, in a good many places, partly covered with vegetation. The whole place literally swarmed with mad priests. The captive pen was back of the palace used by the abbot, but the rescue party had no way of knowing that.

The priests were going here and there, sitting around campfires, stretched on the ground asleep, dancing in front of some old temple, on their knees shouting prayers; some were marching around and around in circles, others walking blindly, not caring who or what they bumped into, their eyes on the moon which was just beginning to come out from behind a cloud.

The mad priests they came close to paid no attention to them. The five soldiers of fortune walked with heads down, and, after the Yid said something, in the old prison lockstep, each man with his hand on the shoulder of the man ahead. His left hand. His right was ready to draw the deadly .45 Colt. Deadly in the hands of men who were all crack shots and unafraid. No more bow and arrow and sword work. From now on it would be shoot until they could shoot no more if they were discovered.

Jimmie Cordie led the parade and, as they got into the formation, said to George Grigsby, the man behind him, "Pass the word that we are going to circulate. If the show-down comes, back to back until we teach them to keep their distance."

Grigsby laughed. "That's the boy, Jimmie."

The lockstep idea of the Yid's was a grand success. It was a new kind of dance to the mad priests who happened to be looking that way when it started. After watching it for a moment or so, several of them at once formed parades of their own. Very soon there were long lines of the mad priests marching around in the lockstep. They started howling and yelling and after a moment or so Jimmie Cordie howled lustily and started a sort of a barbaric chant.

One by one the soldiers of fortune howled also and began to sing. They kept right on howling, only after the first, long drawn out howl they howled gibberish. Grigsby used the only tune he was familiar with, "My Old Kentucky Home." Red, behind Grigsby, used "The Wearing of the Green" for music and always claimed that the words were pure Celtic. The Boston Bean howled "John Brown's Body," as he claimed, in French. The Fighting Yid, not daring to sing in Hebrew, after the experience with the seven mad priests, gave vent very soulfully to "Dere is a happy land, far, far avay. Vere dey eat pork und beans three times a day. Oh! How de boarders yell, ven dey hear it de dinner bell—

three times a day," and so on, in a special kind of pig-Latin. Whatever it all was, all together it made a volume of noise that sounded as if it must issue from very mad priests indeed.

JIMMIE CORDIE LED the way through several of the buildings, winding in and out of the ruins, down streets and around ponds. His thought was to locate some place that looked as if it were being used as a prison or a place where a captive might be guarded. There were priests in all the buildings, some cooking, others eating and sleeping. But in no place was there any sign of a prisoner.

Grigsby, as they filed through a dark place near a wall, stopped howling long enough to say, "It may be, Jimmie, that they do not keep prisoners any longer than—it takes."

"I'm afraid of that, George. It must be getting darn near daylight. Comes the dawn—also comes us getting sunk. We haven't been in a third of the— There's a guard stationed by that door. See, over to the left. In front of that palace. We'll go over. If he tries to halt us, step behind him while I occupy his attention. I guess we can put him out before he squawks."

"You take his attention, Jimmie. I'll see to it that he does not squawk."

The mad priest on guard watched the parade come up, indifferently.

When Jimmie got to within two feet of him, the mad priest stepped squarely in front of Jimmie, his sword drawn back for a thrust. He snarled something in a language Jimmie did not understand. Jimmie howled as if in a rage, then raised both arms high above his head. The mad priest snarled again and advanced his point an inch or so. Jimmie brought his left arm down and clenched his fist. Then he moved the fist slowly to the left, opening one finger at a time. It was an old trick, a very old one used in the West by gunmen to attract the eyes of a man facing them. It worked on the hill of the mad priests of the Kara-Kara sands. The mad priest's eyes followed the hand for a second. Long enough for Grigsby to step out of the line and get almost behind him. The mad priest sensed, rather than saw it, and turned. But it was too late. Grigsby's left arm was around the priest's throat and his right knee in the small of the priest's back.

"Close up, Red," Jimmie commanded calmly. "Cover George."

Red closed up, as did the Bean and the Yid, and then faced out. Between that living wall and the wall of the building a mad priest met his death.

"Push him over in the shadows," Jimmie said as Grigsby lowered the body to the ground. "That's far enough. We'll go in and see what he was guarding."

It was the place where Elizabeth Montague had faced the abbot. The chair he sat on was still on the dais and on the stand were the three jade fish. Near the dais were several of the mad priests—sound asleep.

Jimmie, the first one in, saw them and raised his hand for the howling to cease. The mad priests lay sprawled out in whatever position they were when sleep overcame them. It may have been drugs that put them to sleep or they may have been gorging themselves on food. Several pots half full of something were near them. Whatever the cause, the mad priests were asleep and most of them were snoring.

"Oi, Bean," the Yid said softly, "look at de jade fish. Dey is vorth somethink, I bet you."

"Well," the Bean answered, "put 'em in your pocket, Mr. Cohen."

"I vill do it dot little thing if de pocket of dis robe is big enough und Jimmie marches around de place."

"It doesn't look much like a place where prisoners are kept," Jimmie said. "Those fish are probably some sacred—"

"Jimmie, see that door beyant?" Red interrupted. "Maybeso she is in there, wid this guard and all out here."

"Yeah? Maybeso. I think the guard is for the fish—and some guarding they are doing at the moment. Well, we'll go and take a look. All doors look alike in this man's town."

THEY KEPT CLOSE to the wall, avoiding the sleeping mad priests, and got to the dais. The Yid said, "Vait a minute. I think I take it de jade fish along as a souvenir."

He climbed up on the dais and then started around the chair to get to the table.

"The ruling passion strong in death," Jimmie said with a grin.

The Yid had stooped and pulled something from under the chair. It was the Chinese boy who had translated for the abbot.

The Yid had him by the ankle. The boy opened his mouth to shriek, but before he could draw breath and expel it, the Yid's other hand was over his mouth.

"Quiet," the Yid said sternly but softly.

A whisper carries farther than a low voice, and the Yid remembered it, but he did not remember to speak in anything else but English. He knew several Chinese words and commands, but in remembering one thing he forgot another.

"Hand him down here," Jimmie ordered. "He may know something."

The Yid handed him down to Grigsby and then went on about his business, which at the moment was to get himself a souvenir. The boy was too frightened to even try to yell now. He thought that some of the mad priests had him and were going to torture him. And yet—the mad priests who had pulled him out from under the chair had spoken an English word!

Jimmie Cordie motioned for Grigsby to carry the boy back of the dais, which was fairly long and wide. Once there, Jimmie put a finger to his lips as the boy looked at him, then ordered, "Take your hand away, George. He's all right."

The Yid had not taken his hand from the boy's mouth until Grigsby's hand was ready to substitute.

As Grigsby's hand fell away, Jimmie said, in Pushtu, "Do not be afraid, little brother. We are not going to hurt you."

The boy answered from Grigsby's arms, "I undelstand English. You—you ale not—"

"We are men who have come for one the mad priests hold captive, little brother. Do you—"

"I am also held captive. My father was a mighty, all-pow-elful war lold, and—and the mad pliests slew him and all his men and captuled me. I am the abbot's slave boy. Lescue me, please."

"All right, we will rescue you, also. But first we must rescue a maiden of the English. She was taken when the mad—"

"I know who you mean, mighty one. She is in the captive pen. Tomollow she is to dance on the led hot stones. Dance until she dies in honor of the thlee sacled fish."

"Where is the captive pen?"

"Back of this place. Behind that door the abbot lives, and if he heals us it will be vely bad for us. I sleep most of time under the chair, so that—"

"Tell us all about it later. Can you lead us to the captive pen or are you afraid to do it?"

The boy was intelligent and once his first fright was over and he found out the men who had him were not mad priests, he did not seem to be afraid.

"I am not aflaid. Mad pliests know I go evelywhele. The abbot send me all over. But—five men cannot enter the captive pen. Thele ale many gualds, and they ale not like those monglels who ale supposed to guald the sacled fish. They ale wide awake and—"

"You show us where it is; we'll attend to the guards. Are there guards all around the captive pen?"

"No, only at the gates. Walls all alound. Maybe some-gualds on walls; I don't know."

"We'll find out. What is your name?"

"Li Tang."

"Put Li Tang down, George. Now, you walk beside me, Li Tang. Not to the gate of the captive pen, but to the part of the wall that is farthest away from— You understand me?"

"Sule, luler of the wolld. Plenty undelstand. I lived in Amelican family in Canchow for eight yeals."

"I see. Lead us, then. We will rescue you, also."

7

THE YID'S SACRIFICE

ELIZABETH MONTAGUE LAY asleep just outside her shack, her head pillowed on an arm. Her hand was under her, close to her breast. In it there was clutched the piece of iron band she had seen reflect the rays of the sun. She had worked it loose from the board that held it. The torn, sharp, jagged edge was ready to be drawn across her throat when the mad priests came for her.

She had not intended to go to sleep, but nature intended otherwise.

The moon had come out and it was fairly light, light enough to distinguish figures and faces. She stirred in her sleep as a light tap-tap-tap on her shoulder kept up. At last she opened her eyes and sat up. She saw the Chinese boy kneeling beside her, and as her arm tensed to flash the iron band to her throat she heard a calm voice say in English, "Steady, Montague." The guns have come."

"What? The guns have—" She turned and saw Jimmie Cordie, who had taken off his bonnet. "Who are you?" she asked, just as calmly.

"I am Jimmie Cordie, of the Big Swords, Miss Montague. May I suggest that we defer introductions until after we—"

"Mad pliests coming," warned Li Tang. "I can see them coming flom the gate."

"How many men have you here, Captain Cordie?"

"Four—five counting Li Tang, who is a very good man indeed."

"These priests may be coming for me. If they are, you are not to try to save me. Get back in—"

Jimmie Cordie laughed. "I'll bring up the guns, Miss Montague. Get back here in the shadows. They have turned to the right."

Elizabeth arose and smiled. "I am at your orders, Captain Cordie of the Big Swords."

"Well, those clothes you have on would give us away before we got fifty feet from the wall. Take this robe and bonnet. I'm dark, and—"

"I will take this Chinese boy's robe, cap and slippers. Is he to go with us?"

"Yes, Miss Montague, he is to go with us. But—what will he—"

"My shirt," interrupted Li Tang. "Many times I go alound in it of with nothing on. Mad pliests used to seeing me naked."

"Get behind Captain Cordie where it is dark and take them off. Drop them on the ground and then keep in the darkness until I have put them on. Hurry, boy."

As Li Tang slipped behind Jimmie Cordie, Elizabeth said, "Do you think there is any chance of our making it, Captain Cordie?"

"Well, it is on the knees of the Nine Red Gods. They allowed us to get to you. Maybeso they plan on allowing us to get out. Who knows?"

"You are a fatalist, captain? So am I—to a certain extent. I am—there is something I want to take with me. If the Red Gods plan to allow us to get out, it is of value. I will be back in a moment."

She had remembered the red leather case. It spoke a lot for her nerve, remembering a thing like that in the position she was in. Most women, and men also, would have thought only of escaping from the mad priests.

SHE WENT INTO the hovel and came out in a moment with the case tucked under her left arm. "Have you an extra gun?" she asked.

"No," answered Jimmie, amused at her courage. "Li Tang's outfit is ready, Miss Montague."

Two minutes or less went by, and then Elizabeth stepped from the darkness. She and the Chinese boy were about of the same size and, in the moonlight, if not too close, she did not look unlike him.

"Where is the case you went to get?" Jimmie asked. "Have you forgotten it?"

"No. I put it in the pocket of this robe. If you are ready, Captain Cordie."

"Quite ready," Jimmie answered with a grin. Now that they had found her, unhurt, his spirits had risen once more to their usual gay outlook. "Li Tang, there can't be two of you. If the mad priests see you walking with us and also see you prancing along with a shirt on, what then?"

"I do not know, lesplendent one. Vely selious matter. Vely. No can be two of me."

"Well, we'll make it to the wall and join the rest of the army. It may be we can make a black bonnet out of you as soon as we meet a mad priest who wears, the regalia. You understand what regalia means?"

"No, war lold of all captains."

"I'll tell you some time. Right now, keep between the golden one and me and make yourself as small as possible."

Elizabeth Montague laughed, a gay, amused little laugh. "I have heard a great deal about you, Captain Cordie. Now I know it was not exaggerated. Is Major Grigsby and Red Dolan and—what is it he is called, the—"

"You mean the Boston Bean or the Fighting Yid?"

"Yes. Are they with you, as usual?"

"All of them. They are the army I referred to."

Again Elizabeth laughed. "Well, if Jimmie Cordie, the Fighting Yid, the Boston Bean, Red Dolan and George Grigsby cannot rescue me, who can?"

"You forget Li Tang, here. He is the one who told us where you were, then led us to the wall and had the nerve to climb over with me. He is now an honored member of the outfit, Miss Montague."

"If those Nine Red Gods of yours allow us to escape, I will see to it that he is— But what better reward could he have than to be one of Jimmie Cordie's outfit?"

"Very prettily put, Miss Montague. To the left a little. Isn't it here we came over, Li Tang?"

"Yes, light hele, luler of millions of swolds. But—we wele boosted up. How can we climb up by oulselves?"

"I'll show you. You climb up on my shoulders. You can reach the top with your hands. Can you pull yourself up?"

"Yes, vely easily. I am mole than stlong."

"I'll bet you are. After you get up, roll to the other side

and jump down. Tell Major Grigsby to climb up on the wall with the Fighting Yid."

JIMMIE LIFTED ELIZABETH up to where the Fighting Yid's hands could close on her slender wrists. The Yid's legs were held in a grip like steel by Grigsby.

Once the Yid had her, Elizabeth was on top of the wall in another second. Grigsby lowered the Yid a little and Jimmie Cordie landed beside her.

All four rolled to the other side and jumped down. "What have ye here?" Red demanded. "Where is—"

"Heads up!" shouted the Bean. "Here they come!" And as he shouted his .45 Colt began detonating.

A mad priest had been sleeping partly behind a bale of rotting hemp, close to the wall. The soldiers of fortune had not seen him, and he had neither seen nor heard them when they came up. But a short time later he woke up. He heard Red telling the Yid all about it—in English. Jimmie had warned both of them to keep still, and they had, for a little while.

Grigsby and the Bean were a little farther along the wall. The Yid said something to Red in a low tone. Something about it being duck soup for them, resting while Jimmie Cordie climbed walls. It was kidding, pure and simple; the Yid would have given his eye teeth to be with Jimmie in the captive pen. Red, his cuts hurting him and having a vivid recollection of the Yid's butting in on him when he was playing around with two mads priests, answered in English and just about three tones too loud.

The mad priest listened, puzzled at the language. Grigsby came up and warned Red, who calmed down. The mad priest lay where he was, watching now as well as listening.

He saw Li Tang come over the wall and then saw two of the men climb up. How mad he was cannot be known. Anyway, he was sane enough to realize there was a rescue of some kind going on. Some of the mad priests would have yelled, drawn their sword and charged. This one didn't.

He eased back along the wall and made it to the nearest group of priests, some fifty or sixty. Then he pointed, snarled out something and began dancing up and down in a rage, looking for all the world like an angry chimpanzee. The other priests looked, howled, drew their swords or picked up lances and charged. As they had looked, Jimmie Cordie, Grigsby, the Yid and Elizabeth Montague jumped down from the wall.

Jimmie Cordie looked at them and laughed.

"The rest of the tale will be woe, pure and simple. Let 'em have it! Get in the middle, Montague. You too, Li Tang. Start off, Bean! You next, Yid! Get beside George, Red. I'll rear guard. Spread out a little. Right through and down the hill."

Grigsby smiled as he fired. It was plain to be seen that Jimmie Cordie was back at the old stand. He had found Elizabeth Montague alive and unharmed—and here was a fight to get into.

The heavy bullets sent the mad priests down as a ball send ninepins. They shot a path through the priests—for a little way. Not far. If they had machine guns they could not have shot their way off the hill. The mad priests of Kara-Kara were not afraid of guns or anything else. And there were a thousand times too many of them for any five men to go through.

Jimmie Cordie saw it and ran forward to the Bean. "No can do, Codfish. Head for that building on the left."

THE BUILDING WAS of stone, two stories high, with no windows and with a narrow doorway that would barely admit two slim men at a time. The roof had fallen in at one front corner.

The soldiers of fortune won to it and in. There was no lull in the attack of the mad priests. No sooner had Jimmie Cordie gotten in than two mad priests appeared in the doorway. There was no door. Jimmie turned and shot them both down.

Two more appeared, to fall also. There was a lull while priests were dragging the dead out of the way. A lull, and then two more mad priests charged in, to die in the doorway. The bullets hit them in the face, not the body.

Jimmie Cordie and the Boston Bean held the doorway. The mad priests did not have the chance of a paper cat in the hot place. They came into sight—and bullets from two of the most deadly guns in the Orient met them.

Elizabeth Montague, Red Dolan, the Yid, Grigsby and Li Tang stood by the wall to the right of the doorway. The Yid, Red and Grigsby had their Colt .45s in hand. Elizabeth Montague looked at them and smiled. Dawn had come and, owing to the hole in the roof, it was fairly light in the stone building.

She smiled as she said, "It looks as if we are holed up, gentlemen."

"We are, alanna," answered Red Dolan. "But don't ye worry. The scuts will never take ye from us."

"You are Red Dolan, aren't you?"

"I am. And ye are the English girl that Jimmie was tellin'

me about. What was the matter wid the Chinks that was along to guard ye? Could not they— Where are ye going, ye Yid beneath notice? Stay up wid the rest av us."

The Yid had looked up at the hole and then started along the wall. He halted as Red spoke, and grinned. "I am goink up dere und take a look, Mistake Dolan."

"Up where? Are ye a monkey to climb up the wall? Stay here where ye belong."

"Vatch me und learn somethink, Irish loafer." The Yid jumped, caught the end of a protruding timber, swung himself up, caught another timber farther up and then got his fingers on the flat of a stone that was out of line. He drew his body up, let go one hand, reached up and got hold of the wall where it had once joined the roof. In another second he was head and shoulders out of the hole.

"Bravo, Yid!" called Elizabeth Montague, as if she were at a circus, applauding some clever acrobat.

"Come down from there," Red commanded. "Now I know ye are a monkey, ye—"

The Yid's head appeared. "Tell it to Jimmie dot de main squeeze is earning up. My, is he mad? He is foaming at de mouth und dancink around. Vait till I take it a look." The Yid's head disappeared for a minute, then showed once more. "He is telling de gang somethink. Now dey are all mad as anythink. Dey ain't payink any attention to us. Vait till I take it another look."

"What the hell—I beg the pardon av ye, darlin'—what do we care what the black hearted divils are doin'?" Red called up. "Come down off there, ye Hester Street polecat. Some one will put an arrow in the gullet av ye."

The Yid looked out, then his head appeared.

"Dey is all runnink to von of de buildings. Mit de main squeeze. Somethink is didink."

JIMMIE CORDIE COULD not hear the Yid very well and paid no attention. He was concentrating on the doorway as was the Boston Bean. As the Yid's head came into sight once more the attack ceased.

"Dey are in de building and all around outside it. If dey vasn't mad before, dey are now. Vait till I take it another— I bet you I know what dey is mad about!" He swung down to the dirt floor. "Jimmie, I have thought it of somethink."

"Yeah? Well, some one better think of something before our ammunition gives out. Take my place for a minute, George."

As Grigsby stepped up beside the Bean, Jimmie walked over to the Yid. "All right, Abie. Let's have it."

"You remember ven I took it the jade fish for a souvenir?"

"Yes."

"Vell—know vat dey are, I bet you?"

"I know they are jade fish. What else?"

"Dey are the most precious thing dey have got. Maybeso de fish is vot dey vorship, ain't it?"

"The Fighting Yid is right, Captain Cordie. The jade fish is their god," Elizabeth Montague said. "There is no question about that."

"Maybeso. Go ahead, Yid."

"Vell, I got it dem in my pocket. Here, vait." The Yid took the jade fish from the deep pocket of the black robe. "See dis, kidt?" to Li Tang. "Vot is dey?"

"Oh, my glacious goodness! The thlee sacled fish! The abbot will be mole than clazy now and so will the lest of them. The fish is what they wolship. It is the most sacled thing that—"

"All right, Li Tang. Tell it to us later. What is the idea, Yid?"

"Dis, Jimmie. From de vall I see it another vall I can jump to. From dere I can reach it a big palace und from dere to a pond und from dere to another vall und—"

"From Evers to Tinker to Chance. What of it?"

"Vell, I can go all around in de ruins, I bet you, from roof to roof und so on. Dis of it, I vill get back up dere, yell, und den ven dey look at me, hold up the fish und make it a face at dem. Den I vill jump from de vall on de next von. Vot vill dey do, I esk you?"

"You ask what they will do, Abie? They will let go all holds and chase you over the said walls and roofs and what nots."

"Sure dey vill, all of dem. I vill lead it dem avay across de ruins und vile I am didink it, you can all sneak it down de hill. Vat could be sveeter?"

"Nothing—for us. But a whole heck of a lot of things for you, Mr. Cohen. Did it ever occur to you that they might catch you?"

"Not for a long time dey von't. Den if dey do, vat do I care—you are down de hill mit Miss Montague, ain't it?"

"It is a chance, Abie," Jimmie answered slowly. "A bare, fighting chance. But—"

"Wait a minute, Jimmie," the Yid interrupted, and to the surprise of Elizabeth Montague he spoke perfect English. The soldiers of fortune knew he could, if he wanted to— and if, in his mind, the situation warranted. "There are no buts. I have seen you lead a forlorn hope. I have seen the

Bean lead one. I have seen both George and Red. And once I saw a man we all loved hold a pass until he died so that we might win to safety. We left him because we had a woman to protect—as we have now. Am I unworthy, Jimmie?"

"No, Abie, you are not unworthy. We hold you now as we have held you always, our equal in every respect. You are our partner—I can't say more than that."

"And I," Elizabeth Montague said clearly, "think that you are a gallant gentleman."

"Vell, den," the Yid went back to his usual speech, "dot's plenty. Dere is no time to vaste, ain't it. Ve make it believe dot all de veepink on shoulders is did. Good-by und good luck."

"Abie," Red said. "Ye are not goin' to the death av ye like that, widout—widout—ye know I always loved ye, ye hook-nosed scut av the world."

"Und so did I you, Irish bummer, fell—here goes it nothink. Good-by, George und Beany. I vill be seeink you. Good-by, Jimmie. Und you—"

"Wait," commanded Elizabeth, as the Yid turned to the wall. She walked up to him, took his face between her two hands and kissed him squarely on the mouth. "There are few men, very few, that I have kissed, Yid. I am honored to number you among them in my memory."

"Oi, it is me dot is honored und happy." For once, the soldiers of fortune saw the Fighting Yid embarrassed and showing extreme pleasure at the same time. "Now I fly it over de valls. Von more like dot und I do de chasink, not de mad priests."

Elizabeth kissed the Yid again. "As you said to us— good-by and good luck."

The Yid smiled, jumped for the timber and made it to the top of the wall.

They could not see what he was doing, but they heard him yell. Right afterward they, heard many yells that grew in volume. Then they saw the Yid's legs drawn up to the wall.

"He's gone," Red said. "The Yid—is gone from us. Many is the time I fussed at him and now—"

"Start that later. We may not last ten minutes ourself. Take a look out the door, Bean."

"It is clear to the left," the Bean reported, "for as far as I can see. The mad priests are all running toward— I see the Yid! He is on a roof making faces at them and jumping up and down. They are climbing after him and—he's disappeared."

"Get going," Jimmie commanded curtly. "You and the Bean, George. You next, Miss Montague. Beside her, Li Tang. Beside me, Red. Once more we will try that right through and down the hill thing."

THEY MADE IT—OFF the hill first and then across the sand to the border. The Yid had done what he thought he could do. He put every mad priest on the hill that could walk or run to chasing him to rescue the three jade fish. Nothing else was of the slightest importance to them. If they had seen the party leave the stone house they would not have paid any attention. To them, the fish were all in all—and now in the hands of an enemy!

The journey across the sand was a nightmare. Red's wounds made him give out early, and the Bean and Grigs-by carried him on a seat made by their hands on wrists, Red's arms around their necks.

Then Elizabeth Montague's feet gave out. She had taken off her riding boots to put on Li Tang's slippers at the captive pen and walked in them without a whimper until her feet were raw and bleeding. At last she sat down, saying with a laugh:

"Another casualty, gentlemen. I am afraid I can walk no farther."

"Get on my back," Jimmie commanded, kneeling in front of her, his back to her.

"But, Captain Cordie, I am very heavy."

"No talkee—lidee pigaback, allee same, little girl."

Elizabeth was not very heavy, weighing around one hundred and twenty, but she was no little girl either. Jimmie Cordie stuck it, as did the Bean and Grigsby, but they were all more than glad to take frequent rests before the hills were reached. The soles of Li Tang's feet must have been like shoe leather, because he walked over the sand as if on a bedroom rug.

They cleared the sand just about twenty-four hours after they left the hill. Several times, parties of two and three mad priests were met, heading for the hill. The Bean and Grigsby put Red down and shot the mad priests as they would that many snakes. No mad priest that came close lived to tell about it.

As they stopped near the battlefield in the valley, five thousand Uryankhes Tartars led by Sahet Khan and Zaga-tai came out of the passes and over the mountain ridges.

Jimmie, thinking of the long chance of rescuing the Yid, signaled with a violence that brought the Tartars galloping toward him.

"In a few minutes," Jimmie Cordie said as he knelt so

that Elizabeth Montague could get off his back, "you will have something much better to ride than old man Cordie's son Jimmie."

"I thank you, Jimmie. You also are a very gallant gentleman. I think I will tell you that I—I like you very much."

Jimmie Cordie honestly did not know whether the look in her lovely blue eyes and the tone of her voice rang true—or not. They told that she had fallen in love with him. And yet, Jimmie knew she was—Elizabeth Montague and....

He liked her for her courage and, not being blind, granted the fact that she was very easy on the eyes. But that was as far as it went with him. He realized that she might know that he had the red leather case and was trying to do what Red called "smooch" him.

"I think," he said with a grin, "that if you will honor me as you did the Yid, that will be more than sufficient, Miss Montague."

She looked at him steadily for a moment, then laughed. "It may be that I will—some day, Captain Cordie of the Big Swords. And now, I will take my red leather case, please."

"I am afraid I do not understand. You put it in the pocket of the robe you are wearing, did you not?"

"I did. And when I was rolling over and over on the wall of the captive pen it fell out. You, rolling over and over behind me, picked it up and put it in your pocket."

"Why, so I did. I had forgotten all about it."

"I will take it now."

"If it were yours, I would give it to you, Miss Montague. At that, you may have the case—but not what is in it."

"It is my turn to misunderstand," she said coldly.

"Well, let's see. A Chinese surveyor made some notes.

Some Japs and Russians tried for them. The Japs won and rode away with the notes—which then became stolen notes. You held the Japs up and in turn—I will say confiscated the notes. Whether the mad priests took them away from you and tossed them aside as valueless, I don't know. You dropped them, and I found them. Question, to whom do the notes belong? If the old saying, 'finders keepers,' still is in force, they belong to me."

"You see fit to joke, Captain Cordie. I will take them, please."

SAHET KHAN RODE up. The fierce, dour old Tartar Khan, who could, and did when necessity arose, lead twenty thousand Uryankhes into battle, greeted Jimmie Cordie, who had gone through the ceremony of "blood brother" with him. As soon as he could conclude the greetings, Jimmie asked that a small fire be hastily built. Sahet Khan did not know what Jimmie wanted the fire for, but ordered it built.

Elizabeth Montague stood as if carved out of stone while Jimmie Cordie fed the fire with the survey notes. After it was finished she asked, "Why did you do that, Captain Cordie? They would have been worth a million to either the Soviet or Japan."

"There will be no fighting in the Thian Shan or on either side between the Japanese and the Soviet as long as I can prevent it, Miss Montague. There are too many Manchu and Chinese cities that would be caught between the upper and the nether millstones. And in those cities there are many gentle little women and children."

"I see. As well as being a fatalist, you are also a sentimentalist. I see also that I—made a mistake, Captain Cordie."

"We all do, once in a while, Miss Montague. Now we

will send you on your way with an escort of Uryankhes while we and Sahet Khan go to save the Yid or"—Jimmie's voice grew taut—"avenge him."

A howl that reminded the soldiers of fortune and Elizabeth Montague of the mad priests came from Red Dolan, who was very nearly all right again.

"E-e-e-e-e yah! Look, Jimmie! Look! Tis the Yid! Well, the beneath notice, monkey-faced scut av the world and Hester Street!"

It was the Fighting Yid, nonchalantly strolling up to them. Li Tang squeaked, "My glacious goodness! He has on the abbot's celemonial hat!"

It took some time, after the Yid arrived, to get Red calmed down enough so that the Yid could tell his story. Red patted him on the back, hugged him and did everything but what Elizabeth Montague had done.

The Yid fairly bubbled: "Sure dey chased it me. Over buildings, down vells, across de bottom of de lakes, up in de towers und all over. Ven I got it tired, I hid und rested. My, it vos duck soup keepink avay from dem. Vonce in a vile I put it de fish in my pocket und pulled it de bonnet low und come out und helped dem hunt for me. I vos de chief climber und acrobat for a big—"

"Keep on the main line, Abie," Jimmie interrupted with a grin.

"I vill. Vell, ven night come I met it de abbot comink out of his room. He gave it me de hat for another souvenir."

"He gave it to ye, ye thief av all creation? Ye took it from him and well ye know it," Red stated.

"I did not, Irish bummer. Treat it me mit great respect. I am now de abbot of de mad priests. Git it me madder und

I vill order dot you be skinned alive, red-headt. My, vot a lovely ceremony it vos ven dey made me de—"

"Made ye what? Ye are only a—"

"Save it until later, Red. Come clean, Mr. Cohen."

"Vell, if you put it dot vay, Jimmie. Maybeso de abbot und I had it a little wrestlink match. After it vos over he didn't need it de hat any more, so I put it in my pocket. Den, ven I got good und ready I snuck down de hill und here I am—at de end of a perfect day."

"Day and night, you mean," the Bean corrected. "Well, all's well that ends well. What now, Jeems, me good man? I suggest adjourning to our clothes and then to a spring where we can wash around the ears."

"Vait," the Yid ordered. "I vish to—" He took the three jade fish from his pocket and went up to Elizabeth Montague. As he held them out to her he said, "For a very beautiful lady to remember the Fighting Yid by. He has something of infinitely more value to remember her by."

Elizabeth Montague took the jade fish in her hands. She knew that the three sacred fish of the mad priests of Kara-Kara were worth more to any museum or collector than the survey notes were to the Soviet or Japan, as far as selling for money was concerned.

"Why—why, thank you, Yid. I—it may be that some day I can—"

"Give it me another kiss," the Yid finished for her with a smirk. At that, they all laughed, Elizabeth Montague included.

"Now that everything is settled," Jimmie said, "let's be on our way."

www.ingramcontent.com/pod-product-compliance
Lightning Source LLC
Chambersburg PA
CBHW030532030726
47495CB00004B/954